IN THE HEADLINES

Casualties of War

THE NEW YORK TIMES EDITORIAL STAFF

Published in 2020 by New York Times Educational Publishing
in association with The Rosen Publishing Group, Inc.
29 East 21st Street, New York, NY 10010

First Edition

The New York Times
Caroline Que: Editorial Director, Book Development
Phyllis Collazo: Photo Rights/Permissions Editor
Heidi Giovine: Administrative Manager

Rosen Publishing
Megan Kellerman: Managing Editor
Michael Hessel-Mial: Editor
Greg Tucker: Creative Director
Brian Garvey: Art Director

Cataloging-in-Publication Data
Names: New York Times Company.
Title: Casualties of war / edited by the New York Times editorial staff.
Description: New York : The New York Times Educational Publish-
ing, 2020. | Series: In the headlines | Includes glossary and index.
Identifiers: ISBN 9781642823035 (library bound) | ISBN
9781642823028 (pbk.) | ISBN 9781642823042 (ebook)
Subjects: LCSH: Civilian war casualties—Juvenile literature. |
Civilians in war—Juvenile literature. | War—Moral and ethical
aspects—Juvenile literature. | Military history, Modern—20th
century—Case studies—Juvenile literature. | Military history,
Modern—21st century—Case studies—Juvenile literature.
Classification: LCC U21.2 C378 2020 | DDC 363.34'98—dc23

Manufactured in the United States of America

On the cover: A wounded man is carried following an airstrike
in Syria on the rebel-held besieged town of Arbin, in the eastern
Ghouta region on the outskirts of the capital Damascus, Jan. 2,
2018; Abdulmonam Eassa/AFP/Getty Images.

Contents

CHAPTER 3

Rape and Torture as Weapons of War

CHAPTER 4

The Humanitarian Impact of War

CHAPTER 5

Lives Unsettled by Occupation and Displacement

CHAPTER 6

Remembering and Reckoning With the Aftermath

Introduction

CARL VON CLAUSEWITZ famously called war "politics by other means," implying that war is a tool, a necessary evil to advance a goal. In addition, war is easy to romanticize. We imagine acts of heroism in movies, tactical brilliance in history books, a skillful sequence of kills in a video game and only occasionally the large, unfortunate numbers that accompany them: the victims. In the end, the victims pay war's ultimate price.

The traditional picture of war, where professional armies contend on an empty battlefield, has been replaced by unconventional warfare. In this model of war, high-tech militaries and low-tech guerrillas battle right where civilians live, in the crosshairs.

There are dozens of armed conflicts taking place at this very moment. These wars may seem distant even though the United States and other powerful nations play a strong role in them. To grasp the real effects of war, it is necessary to turn to the victims. By focusing on them, we gain a stronger understanding of war's systematic destruction. War invariably exposes civilians to the threat of mass killings, torture, rape, famine, disease and displacement. Even democratic nations with professional volunteer armies are capable of committing atrocities, as the articles in this collection show.

A challenge to war reporting is that there are significant barriers to fact-finding. Battle sites can be off-limits to reporters, and military policies are often not shared with the public. Even finding the number of casualties is a challenge, let alone determining if war crimes have been committed. Often, unsubstantiated reports are confirmed only years later. As a result, carefully following the complex lines of reporting is essential to uncovering atrocities as they take place.

War's economic impact creates additional victims. Fundamentally, war disrupts the ordinary workings of people's lives, leading to crises that would be preventable in peacetime. Blocked grain transportation, a contaminated water supply or the collapse of public services can easily add famine or disease to a war's horrors. Today, most humanitarian crises occur when military conflict causes such disruptions. Such devastation is often the result of deliberate policy, as in the case of Saudi Arabia's war against Yemen.

As conflicts unfold, civilian lives are further disrupted by twin problems that affect freedom of movement: displacement and occupation. Most visible to us is displacement. Recent conflicts in the Middle East have led to millions of refugees seeking asylum elsewhere in the world. A look back at the history of war shows us just how common this phenomenon can be. But behind displacement is the threat to people's livelihoods that comes from long-term military occupations.

Years after the last shot has been fired, survivors of war remain haunted by what they have experienced. However, survivors have often led in building institutions that help countries prevent or recover from the horrors of war. After a series of devastating conflicts in the 1990s, many organizations improved their responses to war crimes and humanitarian crises. Mostly powerfully, Rwanda, devastated by a genocidal civil war, developed a new grassroots model of national reconciliation. Rwanda's grassroots justice system helped victims of genocide nonviolently pursue justice against perpetrators, person to person, and rebuild the social trust that was shattered during wartime.

In Gandhi's writings, he observes that while history is defined by war, the long-term survival of humanity has always depended on its tools for mutual coexistence. While the world's conflicts are unlikely to suddenly end, these articles remind us of the choices we can make in how we wage war. Armies can limit the incidence of abuse, just as they can choose not to exacerbate famines. People can support

People lined up for food rations being distributed under military watch in Mainok village in Borno State, Nigeria, Feb. 11, 2017. Dozens of cases of rape, sexual violence and sexual exploitation carried out by guards, camp officials, security officers and members of civilian vigilante groups were reported in Borno State in 2016.

international institutions that promote diplomacy and rules of conduct. And most importantly, governments can choose not to escalate a conflict. Such long-term thinking may one day help us imagine a world without war.

CHAPTER 1

Rich Nations Pursue War at a Distance

Although the United States is currently using military force in a number of countries, most Americans remain unaffected at home. This distance is partly due to the changing character of war, as the use of airstrikes and special forces has become more common. Other wealthy nations, allies and enemies alike, share this tendency to wage war from afar. In addition, the United States and other nations boast significant arms sales, making these distant wars considerably profitable. The cumulative effect has been to make the scope of casualties invisible to the American public.

Drones and the Democracy Disconnect

OPINION | BY FIRMIN DEBRABANDER | SEPT. 14, 2014

WITH PRESIDENT OBAMA'S announcement that we will open a new battlefront in yet another Middle Eastern country — in Syria, against ISIS (the Islamic State in Iraq and Syria) — there is widespread acknowledgment that it will be a protracted, complex, perhaps even messy campaign, with many unforeseeable consequences along the way. The president has said we will put "no boots on the ground" in Syria; he is wary of simply flooding allies on the ground with arms, for fear that they will fall into the wrong hands — as they already have. Obama wants to strike against ISIS in a part of Syria that is currently outside the authority of the Syrian government, which the president has accused of war crimes, and is thus, in our eyes, a legal no-man's land. He has also made clear that he is ready to go it alone in directing attacks on ISIS — he has asked for Congress's support, but is not seeking their authorization. All these signs point to drones playing a prominent role in this new war in Syria.

Increasingly, this is how the United States chooses to fight its wars. Drones lead the way and dominate the fight against the several non-state actors we now engage — Al Qaeda, the Shabab in Somalia and now ISIS. Drones have their benefits: They enable us to fight ISIS without getting mired on the ground or suffering casualties, making them politically powerful and appealing. For the moment, the American public favors striking ISIS; that would likely change if our own ground forces were involved.

If any group deserves drone strikes, it may well be ISIS.

This fundamentalist Muslim group, so brutal that even Al Qaeda shunned it, has taken to forcibly converting and exterminating Christians and other minority religious groups; one such minority, the Yazidis, may have narrowly escaped genocide at ISIS' hands. The West has received vivid proof of the group's ferocity. On Saturday it released its third video of a beheading — this time of a British aid worker — after two other such videos of the beheadings of American journalists within the past month.

The use of drones raises not just strategic and political problems, but ethical questions as well. In particular, what does our use of and reliance on drones say about us? How do drones affect the nation that endorses them — overtly, or, as is more often the case, tacitly? Are drones compatible with patriotism? With democracy? Honor? Glory? Or do they, as I fear, represent — and exacerbate — a troubling, even obscene disconnect between the American people and the wars waged in our name?

Writing in The Guardian in 2012, George Monbiot declared the United States' drone strikes in Pakistan cowardly. He echoed the howls of many Pakistanis on the ground, who suffer the drone onslaught firsthand, while those who carry it out are safely removed thousands of miles away. The new breed of warriors is strange indeed: They are safely ensconced here in the United States, often commuting to work like ordinary citizens, and after a day spent monitoring and perhaps striking enemy targets, they return home to kids, homework and dinner.

Drone apologists, and many defense experts, claim drones are a reasonable development in warfare technology. The Slate commentator Jamie Holmes argues that extreme complaints about military innovations are hardly new. To people like Monbiot, or the BBC commentator Jeremy Clarkson, who scoffs that medals for drone pilots "should feature an armchair and a Coke machine or two crossed burgers," Holmes says, "the hyperventilating about heroism being killed by machines misses the point. For one, the list of weapons once considered 'cowardly' ... include[s] not only the submarines of World War I but also the bow and arrow and the gun. The point of each of these technologies was the same: to gain an asymmetrical advantage against adversaries and reduce risk."

There are few philosophers more clear-eyed, frank, even cynical when it comes to war than Niccolò Machiavelli. In "The Prince," he asserts that war is inescapable, inevitable. He praises the Romans for understanding the danger in putting it off. To the simple question of when you should go to war, Machiavelli's simple answer is, "When you can" — not when it is just, or "right." And yet, in another work, "The Art of War," Machiavelli reveals that *how* a nation goes to war, *how* a nation chooses to fight is just as critical, perhaps even more so. At this point, the issue of military technology is pertinent, and Machiavelli's discussion of the topic is highly reminiscent of our current debate about drones and character.

In "The Art of War," Machiavelli again praises the ancient Romans, for their battlefield exploits, and states his worry that newly introduced artillery "prevents men from employing and displaying their virtue as they used to do of old." Machiavelli ultimately dismisses such fears — though he was only contemplating cannons at the time. But elsewhere he declares that "whoever engages in war must use every means to put himself in a position of facing his enemy in the field and beating him there," since a field war "is the most necessary and honorable of all wars." Why is this? Because on the battlefield, military discipline and courage are exhibited and forged, and your opponent gets a true taste of what he's up against — not only the army, but the nation he is up against.

For Machiavelli, military conduct is a reflection, indeed an extension — better yet, the *root* and foundation of a nation's character, the bravery and boldness of its leaders, the devotion and determination of its citizens. Military conduct is indelibly linked to civic virtue, which is why he argues that nations should reject a professional army, much less a mercenary one, in favor of a citizen militia. Every citizen must get a taste of military discipline — and sacrifice. Every citizen must have a stake, an intimate investment, in the wars his nation fights.

Machiavelli was highly sensitive to the role military glory plays in inspiring the public and uniting, even defining, a nation. Great battles and military campaigns forged the identity, cohesion and indomitable pride of the Roman Republic, Machiavelli maintains — across the different social classes — and stoked the democratic energy of the people. Haven't they served a similar purpose in our own republic? War has offered iconic images of our national identity: George Washington crossing the Delaware with his ragtag soldiers; marines hoisting the flag at Iwo Jima. These images are inherently democratic — they offer no king on his steed, lording over kneeling troops. To that extent, they nourish and reinforce our democratic identity and sensibilities.

This is no longer the case in the age of drones. I have strained to imagine the great battles drones might fight, which the public might rally around and solemnly commemorate. But this is a silly proposition — which cuts to the heart of the matter.

Never have the American people been more removed from their wars, even while we are the most martial nation on earth, and drones are symptoms, and drivers, of this troubling alienation. The United

States has been engaged in two expensive and protracted wars in the past decade, as well as the seemingly endless war on terror spread the world over. The war in Afghanistan — where drones have made their mark as never before — is the longest in the nation's history, and we have spent more money rebuilding Afghanistan than we did on Europe after World War II. Through all our recent wars in the region, however, most Americans have hardly felt a thing. Given the extent of our military engagement, unparalleled in the world, that is astounding, shameful even, and politically treacherous.

Critics have long warned that drones put too much warmaking power in the hands of few government actors, who increasingly operate on their own, or in the shadows. Many felt we saw a preview of political abuses to come when President Obama unilaterally ordered a drone strike against an American citizen in Yemen. This new technology has already emboldened our government to openly wage war in countries against which we have not officially declared war. We operate there with the tacit, and dubious, assent of a few ruling interests.

Perhaps it is not inevitable that drones are linked to arbitrary, centralized government; perhaps drone warfare can be waged transparently, democratically, legally, though it is admittedly hard to imagine what that would look like. What is certain, however, is that drone technology offers manifold temptations to those who would expand the borders of our wars, or wage war according to their own agenda, independent of the will, or interest, or attention of the American public.

Most American citizens are quick to let someone or something else bear the brunt of our wars, and take up the fight. Hence there is less worry about whether a given incursion is necessary, justified, logical or humane. Drones point to a new and terrible kind of cruelty — violence far removed from the perpetrator, and easier to inflict in that regard. With less skin in the game — literally — we can be less vigilant about the darker tendencies of our leaders, the unintended consequences of their actions, and content to indulge in private matters.

The United State is gradually becoming a warring nation with fewer and fewer warriors, and few who know the sacrifices of war. Drones represent the new normal, and are an easy invitation to enter into and wage war — indefinitely. This is a state of affairs Machiavelli could not abide by, and neither should we. It is antithetical to a democracy for its voting public to be so aloof from the wars it fights. It is a feature, I fear, of a democracy destined to lose that title.

FIRMIN DEBRABANDER, an associate professor of philosophy at the Maryland Institute College of Art, Baltimore, is the author of "Spinoza and the Stoics" and a forthcoming book critiquing the gun rights movement.

Sentences in Blackwater Killings Give Iraqis a Measure of Closure

BY OMAR AL-JAWOSHY AND TIM ARANGO | APRIL 14, 2015

BAGHDAD — Ali Khalaf, a traffic police officer, stood in busy Nisour Square on Tuesday, waving the cars by, and pointed.

"It was there," he said, "where people were dying and bleeding without reason. Blackwater vehicles were there, and its soldiers were shooting at people without pity."

He added, "It was as if I was watching a horror movie."

Mr. Khalaf, 42, was a witness to the killings of 17 Iraqis in the square, almost eight years ago, by guards for the private security company Blackwater, who were under contract with the State Department. The F.B.I. found that 14 of the killings were unjustified and violated deadly-force rules for contractors, and on Monday, four of the guards were sentenced to long prison terms — one of them for life, the others for 30 years — by a federal judge in Washington. The sentencing afforded Mr. Khalaf and other Iraqis who were traumatized by the deadly episode a chance at closure.

"I'm very happy to hear of this verdict against those criminals who killed innocent Iraqis without mercy," Mr. Khalaf said.

The Blackwater killings joined two other high-profile atrocities, the Abu Ghraib prison torture scandal and the massacre of civilians by Marines in Haditha, in destroying the credibility of the long American occupation in the eyes of Iraqis.

Nevertheless, the Iraqi news media took little notice of the convictions, perhaps because there are so many present-day traumas to cover: the fight against the Islamic State; a car bomb that blew up Tuesday morning near a Baghdad hospital, killing five people; and a bomb in the south of the capital that killed an additional seven civilians. Some of those interviewed here on Tuesday learned of the news from the BBC and the Arabiya television networks.

Underscoring Iraq's seemingly never-ending traumas, the sentences were handed down at a time of renewed American military involvement in the country to fight the extremists of the Islamic State. Prime Minister Haider al-Abadi arrived in Washington on Tuesday to meet with President Obama, and to ask for more weapons and airstrikes against the insurgents.

But the sentences close a painful chapter for the Iraqis whose lives were upended by the tragedy.

This being Iraq, where notions of revenge and eye-for-an-eye justice run deep, many people felt the sentences were too lenient. Many, including Mr. Khalaf, the traffic police officer, said the contractors deserved to die.

Saddam Jawad, 32, who lost his mother that day, agreed. "They should have been sentenced to death," he said. Still, he added, "I was relieved when I heard of the resolution."

While the sentences may have provided a measure of justice that many Iraqis doubted would ever be done, they also revived painful memories.

"I won't forget my mother and the terrible scenes of burning, blood and dead people at the square," Mr. Jawad said. "They killed my mother, the dearest person in my life. I won't forgive them."

Firas Fadhil, 52, broke down in tears on Tuesday when he recalled the brother he had lost in the shootout. He, too, said the sentences for the contractors — who asserted their innocence in court — were too light.

"This is a very important resolution, but they must be murdered, as they killed our people without feeling guilty," he said. "American justice must sentence them to death. They must be sentenced to death. I lost my brother, and nothing will ever compensate me for his death."

The massacre happened on Sept. 16, 2007, when a convoy of Blackwater vehicles entered the square and security guards, believing an insurgent attack was underway, began shooting at people indiscriminately.

The episode, which occurred at the height of the American military involvement in Iraq and while the insurgency was still strong, became a dark chapter of the occupation and turned many Iraqis against the Americans. It also highlighted the heavy reliance of the United States government on security contractors, whom many Iraqis had come to loathe as cowboys operating outside the bounds of the law.

One reason the killings did such damage to the standing of the United States was the widespread belief among Iraqis that the American justice system would never hold anyone accountable.

"There was a lack of confidence between the Iraqi people and the United States administration," said Abbas al-Mussawi, a spokesman for Vice President Nuri Kamal al-Maliki, who was prime minister at the time of the shootings. "I think this verdict will help restore confidence."

Abdul Amir was shot four times in the leg during that chaotic day but escaped with his life. He criticized the "slowness" of American justice, but praised the fact that there was finally a resolution.

Even so, he said, he will be scarred for life.

"They are painful memories," he said. "I always remember the spot where I was bleeding. I watch that movie in my mind every time I pass through the square."

OMAR AL-JAWOSHY reported from Baghdad, and **TIM ARANGO** from Istanbul.

Block the Sale of Warplanes to Nigeria

EDITORIAL | BY THE NEW YORK TIMES | MAY 18, 2016

FOURTEEN MONTHS AFTER the election of President Muhammadu Buhari in Nigeria, the Obama administration is considering selling his government 12 warplanes. It is a thorny decision because Mr. Buhari is an improvement over his disastrous predecessor, Goodluck Jonathan, and is fighting Boko Haram, the Islamist extremists who have terrorized the region. But he has not done enough to end corruption and respond to charges that the army has committed war crimes in its fight against the group. Selling him the planes now would be a mistake.

Under Mr. Buhari, Nigeria has cooperated more with Chad and Niger to fight Boko Haram. The group, which emerged in the early 2000s, has seized land in the northeastern, predominantly Muslim section of Nigeria. Thousands of people have been killed and 2.2 million displaced. The group's depravity captured world attention in 2014 when it kidnapped 276 girls from a secondary school.

While violence is down and some territory has been recaptured, the group continues to attack remote villages and refugee camps, and it is using women and children as suicide bombers. American military officials say that Boko Haram has begun collaborating with the Islamic State and that the groups could be planning attacks on American allies in Africa.

Yet Nigeria's government cannot be entrusted with the versatile new warplanes, which can be used for ground attacks as well as reconnaissance. Its security services have long engaged in extrajudicial killings, torture and rape, according to the State Department's latest annual human rights report. Amnesty International says that during the army's scorched-earth response to Boko Haram between 2011 and 2015, more than 8,200 civilians were murdered, starved or tortured to death.

The Obama administration was so concerned about this record that two years ago it blocked Israel's sale of American-made Cobra attack helicopters to Nigeria and ended American training of Nigerian troops. American officials even hesitated to share intelligence with the military, fearing it had been infiltrated by Boko Haram. That wariness has eased and American officials say they are now working with some Nigerian counterparts.

Since winning election on a reform platform, Mr. Buhari has moved to root out graft and to investigate human rights abuses by the military. But the State Department said Nigerian "authorities did not investigate or punish the majority of cases of police or military abuse" in 2015.

That hardly seems like an endorsement for selling the aircraft. Tim Rieser, a top aide to Senator Patrick Leahy, who wrote the law barring American aid to foreign military units accused of abuses, told The Times that "we don't have confidence in the Nigerians' ability to use them in a manner that complies with the laws of war and doesn't end up disproportionately harming civilians, nor in the capability of the U.S. government to monitor their use."

To defeat Boko Haram, which preys on citizens' anger at the government, Mr. Buhari will need more than weapons. He has to get serious about improving governance and providing jobs, roads and services in every region of Nigeria. Until then or until Congress develops ways to monitor the planes' use, it should block the sale.

At a 'Defense' Expo, an Antiseptic World of Weaponry

BY BEN HUBBARD | FEB. 23, 2017

ABU DHABI, UNITED ARAB EMIRATES — Serbia showed off armored vehicles, rockets and rifles, and drew in passers-by with a video showing soldiers shooting targets to action movie music.

Pakistan had glass cases full of bullets, mortars, grenades and guns, including a gold-plated AK-47.

And Sudan displayed an antiaircraft missile and its launcher. A salesman in a white robe and snakeskin shoes pointed out that it was an upgraded model.

"Now they have a wider area of explosion," he said proudly.

Such casual sales pitches for lethal merchandise coursed through the carpeted halls of this wealthy Arab city's convention center this week, when more than 1,200 military technology companies and contractors from around the world convened to hawk their wares.

The event, the International Defense Exhibition and Conference, or IDEX, is the largest show of its kind in the Middle East, and it had the feel of a high-end arms bazaar, a megamall where men in dark suits browsed Estonian drones, Chinese tanks, Brazilian amphibious vehicles and guns from all over.

There was so much weaponry inside that visitors were searched not just on the way in, but also on the way out.

The exhibition served to promote Abu Dhabi, the capital of the United Arab Emirates, which has distinguished itself as a regional hub for international business at a time when wars and uprisings have upended other Arab states.

It also provided a visual layout of the global arms trade, which is at its most active since the end of the Cold War, analysts say.

International transfers of major weapons over the last five years were 8.3 percent higher than during the previous five-year period, the Stockholm International Peace Research Institute said in a recent report.

Much of that traffic was in the Middle East, where wars are raging in Syria, Iraq, Libya and Yemen, and where Persian Gulf states like Saudi Arabia have beefed up their arsenals because of worries about Iran.

Arms deals worth more than $5.2 billion were announced during the five-day event, which ended on Thursday, according to Gulf News.

Regional and international realities lurked not far below the glittering surface.

The United States had the most floor space, befitting its status as the world's largest arms exporter. More than 100 American companies were present, with elaborate displays showing everything from handguns to armored vehicles to drones.

Iran, referred to by one defense executive as "the big guy across the strait," was not invited. Nor was Israel, another major weapons producer.

But dozens of other countries were, highlighting how many have expanded their arms exports to earn money and build alliances.

Many at the show noted the size of the Chinese display, where eight state-run companies advertised boats, tanks, missiles and other items. Standing next to a real-life tank, Ji Yanzhao, deputy director for marketing at Norinco, said that his company was targeting the Middle Eastern market, which is why it had brought not one but two armored vehicles to display.

"The real thing always does better than the models," he said, as another visitor smiled for a photo with the tank.

Tate Nurkin, senior director for strategic assessments at IHS Jane's, said that many middle-income countries had entered the arms business over the last decade and now provided lower-cost alternatives for states on tight budgets.

That list has expanded recently in the Middle East, where low oil prices have left some Arab states looking for bargains where previously they snapped up top-of-the-line items.

"They don't need to buy just American high-end equipment," Mr. Nurkin said. "They can buy from China, and it's good enough."

As a Middle East correspondent, during visits to Gaza, Syria, Iraq and Yemen I have seen up close the human cost to communities on the receiving end of many of these weapons. So after a few hours of wandering between displays, I began feeling overwhelmed.

They ranged in size and approach, but the marketing language focused on "defense," as if none of the weapons could be used to invade one's neighbor, break up families or create refugees.

Nowhere did I see images of blood, injuries or death.

"It's a very dangerous world and region, and there are things worth defending, and that requires some of this equipment," Mr. Nurkin said. "But it can be a bit disconcerting for those who have never been to defense exhibitions to see them being traded like iPhones."

Poongsan, a South Korean company, had bullets of different sizes arranged in lighted glass cases, like jewelry. Glock, the Austrian gun maker, had more than a dozen pistols out for visitors to cock, aim and take selfies with, making it one of the most visited stalls.

"It's because we have the best goodies," a woman behind the counter explained before correcting herself. "The best *products*."

Many of the marketing slogans made sense only if you knew what the product did.

"Sees with out being seen," boasted an ad for a Czech-made radar system.

"Your aim is our target," promised a company displaying swiveling targets for marksmanship.

"Nothing escapes you," said an ad for an optics company that makes, among other things, rifle scopes.

Sudan's section featured a two-story fake stone castle surrounded by displays of rifles, rockets and a large, gray GPS-guided bomb.

"It is a very accurate way to hit a target," said Ibrahim Ismael Bashir, the sales and marketing director for Sudan's Military Industry Corporation.

In a small room nearby, I picked up a Sudanese machine gun simulator and blasted away at targets on a screen as martial ballads played in the background.

One of the most photographed items was a gold-plated AK-47 displayed by Pakistan. Muhammad Iqbal, the technical manager for weapons at the Pakistan Ordnance Factories, said the rifle cost about $1,000 and was usually bought by collectors or presented to foreign dignitaries, especially from the Middle East.

"They are very fond of this," he said.

But the show was not all about weapons.

"Come on, I'll show you the robot," said Paul Bosscher, the chief engineer for robotic systems at Harris, of Melbourne, Fla., which focuses on communication technology.

On display was the company's new robot, T7, which stands about six feet tall, moves about on treads and has a single arm with a big metal pincer on the end. Armored, covered with cameras and controlled remotely, it was designed to defuse bombs and, the company hopes, save lives — not just of civilians but also the soldiers and the police who have to cope with the explosives.

As I gripped the controller and directed the robot to stack lengths of plastic pipe, a man posed next to it while his friend took a photo.

"Who doesn't want to get their photo with a robot?" Mr. Bosscher said.

Arms Sales to Saudis Leave American Fingerprints on Yemen's Carnage

BY DECLAN WALSH AND ERIC SCHMITT | DEC. 25, 2018

CAIRO — When a Saudi F-15 warplane takes off from King Khalid air base in southern Saudi Arabia for a bombing run over Yemen, it is not just the plane and the bombs that are American.

American mechanics service the jet and carry out repairs on the ground. American technicians upgrade the targeting software and other classified technology, which Saudis are not allowed to touch. The pilot has likely been trained by the United States Air Force.

And at a flight operations room in the capital, Riyadh, Saudi commanders sit near American military officials who provide intelligence and tactical advice, mainly aimed at stopping the Saudis from killing Yemeni civilians.

American fingerprints are all over the air war in Yemen, where errant strikes by the Saudi-led coalition have killed more than 4,600 civilians, according to a monitoring group. In Washington, that toll has stoked impassioned debate about the pitfalls of America's alliance with Saudi Arabia under Crown Prince Mohammed bin Salman, who relies on American support to keep his warplanes in the air.

Saudi Arabia entered the war in 2015, allying with the United Arab Emirates and a smattering of Yemeni factions with the goal of ousting the Iran-allied Houthi rebels from northern Yemen. Three years on, they have made little progress. At least 60,000 Yemenis have died in the war, and the country stands on the brink of a calamitous famine.

For American officials, the stalled war has become a strategic and moral quagmire. It has upended the assumptions behind the decades-old policy of selling powerful weapons to a wealthy ally that, until recently, rarely used them. It has raised questions about complicity in possible war crimes. And the civilian toll has posed a troubling dilemma: how to support Saudi allies while keeping the war's excesses at arm's length.

In interviews, 10 current and former United States officials portrayed a troubled and fractious American response to regular reports of civilians killed in coalition airstrikes.

The Pentagon and State Department have denied knowing whether American bombs were used in the war's most notorious airstrikes, which have struck weddings, mosques and funerals. However, a former senior State Department official said that the United States had access to records of every airstrike over Yemen since the early days of the war, including the warplane and munitions used.

At the same time, American efforts to advise the Saudis on how to protect civilians often came to naught. The Saudis whitewashed an American-sponsored initiative to investigate errant airstrikes and often ignored a voluminous no-strike list.

"In the end, we concluded that they were just not willing to listen," said Tom Malinowski, a former assistant secretary of state and an incoming member of Congress from New Jersey. "They were given specific coordinates of targets that should not be struck and they continued to strike them. That struck me as a willful disregard of advice they were getting."

Yet American military support for the airstrikes continued.

While American officials often protested civilian deaths in public, two presidents ultimately stood by the Saudis. President Obama gave the war his qualified approval to assuage Saudi anger over his Iran nuclear deal. President Trump embraced Prince Mohammed and bragged of multibillion-dollar arms deals with the Saudis.

As bombs fell on Yemen, the United States continued to train the Royal Saudi Air Force. In 2017, the United States military announced a $750 million program focused on how to carry out airstrikes, including avoiding civilian casualties. The same year, Congress authorized the sale of more than $510 million in precision-guided munitions to Saudi Arabia, which had been suspended by the Obama administration in protest of civilian casualties.

Nearly 100 American military personnel are advising or assisting the coalition war effort, although fewer than 35 are based in Saudi Arabia.

American support for the war met stiff headwinds this fall, when congressional fury over the murder of the Saudi dissident Jamal Khashoggi combined with worries over civilian deaths in Yemen.

In response, the Trump administration ended American air-to-air refueling of coalition warplanes over Yemen in November but has otherwise continued to support the war. This month, the Senate voted to end American military assistance to the war altogether, a sharp rebuke to the Trump administration, but the bill died when the House refused to consider it.

The civilian toll is still rising. According to the Armed Conflict Location and Event Data Project, November was the most violent month in Yemen since the group began tracking casualties in January 2016. There were 3,058 war-related fatalities in November, it said, including 80 civilians killed in airstrikes.

'EXPENSIVE PAPERWEIGHTS'

For decades, the United States sold tens of billions of dollars in arms to Saudi Arabia on an unspoken premise: that they would rarely be used.

The Saudis amassed the world's third-largest fleet of F-15 jets, after the United States and Israel, but their pilots almost never saw action. They shot down two Iranian jets over the Persian Gulf in 1984, two Iraqi warplanes during the 1991 gulf war and they conducted a handful of bombing raids along the border with Yemen in 2009.

The United States had similar expectations for its arms sales to other Persian Gulf countries.

"There was a belief that these countries wouldn't end up using this equipment, and we were just selling them expensive paperweights," said Andrew Miller, a former State Department official now with the Project on Middle East Democracy.

Then came Prince Mohammed bin Salman.

When the prince, then the Saudi defense minister, sent fighter jets to Yemen in March 2015, Pentagon officials were flustered to receive just 48 hours notice of the first strikes against Houthi rebels, two former

President Trump, meeting with Crown Prince Mohammed bin Salman of Saudi Arabia in March, bragged of American arms sales to the kingdom.

senior American officials said. American officials were persuaded by Saudi assurances the campaign would be over in weeks.

But as the weeks turned to years, and the prospect of victory receded, the Americans found themselves backing a military campaign that was exacting a steep civilian toll, largely as a result of Saudi and Emirati airstrikes.

American military officials posted to the coalition war room in Riyadh noticed that inexperienced Saudi pilots flew at high altitudes to avoid enemy fire, military officials said. The tactic reduced the risk to the pilots but transferred it to civilians, who were exposed to less accurate bombings.

Coalition planners misidentified targets and their pilots struck them at the wrong time — destroying a vehicle as it passed through a crowded bazaar, for instance, instead of waiting until it reached an open road. The coalition routinely ignored a no-strike list — drawn up by the United States Central Command and the United Nations — of hospitals, schools and other places where civilians gathered.

At times, coalition officers subverted their own chain of command. In one instance, a devastating strike that killed 155 people in a funeral hall was ordered by a junior officer who countermanded an order from a more senior officer, a State Department official said.

The Americans offered help. The State Department financed an investigative body to review errant airstrikes and propose corrective action. Pentagon lawyers trained Saudi officers in the laws of war. Military officers suggested putting gun cameras on Saudi and Emiratis warplanes to see how strikes were being conducted. The coalition balked.

In June 2017, American officials extracted new promises of safeguards, including stricter rules of engagement and an expansion of the no-strike list to about 33,000 targets — provisions that allowed the secretary of state, then Rex W. Tillerson, to win support in Congress for the sale of more than $510 million in precision-guided munitions to the kingdom.

But those measures seemed to make little difference. Just over a year later, in August 2018, a coalition airstrike killed at least 40 boys on a packed school bus in northern Yemen.

Still, American leaders insisted they need to keep helping the Saudi coalition.

America's role in the war was "absolutely essential" to safeguard civilians, the general in charge of Central Command, Gen. Joseph L. Votel, told a charged Senate hearing in March.

"I think this does give us the best opportunity to address these concerns," he said.

WHAT THE U.S. KNOWS

In March, Prince Mohammed paid a visit to Washington, where he was feted by President Trump. As the two leaders sat in the White House, Mr. Trump held aloft a chart with price-tagged photos of warplanes and other weapons.

"$3 billion," Mr. Trump said, pointing to the chart. "$533 million. $525 million. That's peanuts for you."

The prince chuckled.

But in Congress, the mood was souring. In the March hearing, senators accused the Pentagon of being complicit in the coalition's errant bombing, and pressed its leaders on how directly the United States was linked to atrocities.

General Votel said the military knew little about that. The United States did not track whether the coalition jets that it refueled carried out the airstrikes that killed civilians, he said, and did not know when they used American-made bombs. At a briefing in Cairo in August, a senior United States official echoed that assessment.

"I would assume the Saudis have an inventory system that traces that information," said the official, who spoke anonymously to discuss diplomatically sensitive relations. "But that's not information that is available to the U.S."

But Larry Lewis, a State Department adviser on civilian harm who worked with the Saudi-led coalition from 2015 to 2017, said that information was readily available from an early stage.

At the coalition headquarters in Riyadh, he said, American liaison officers had access to a database that detailed every airstrike: warplane, target, munitions used and a brief description of the attack. American officials frequently emailed him copies of a spreadsheet for his own work, he said.

The data could easily be used to pinpoint the role of American warplanes and bombs in any single strike, he said. "If the question was "Hey, was that a U.S. munition they used?" You would know that it was," he said.

Capt. Bill Urban, a spokesman for Central Command, did not deny the existence of the database, but said that American officers only used coalition data to carry out their core mission: advising on civilian casualties, sharing intelligence on Houthi threats and coordinating the midair refueling that ended in November.

"I will not speculate on how the United States could have used or compiled the information the Saudi-led coalition shared for some other function," he said in a statement. "That is not the mission these advisers were invited to Riyadh to perform. That is not the way partnerships work."

Other officials have said that collating information about use of American munitions in Yemen would be onerous and, ultimately, pointless. "What difference would it make?" the senior United States official in Cairo said.

But legal experts say such information could be significant. Inside the State Department, there have been longstanding worries about potential legal liability for the American role in the war. In August, the United Nations' human rights body determined that some coalition airstrikes were likely war crimes.

Under American law, customers of American weapons must follow the laws of armed conflict or future sales may be blocked, said Ryan Goodman, a former Defense Department attorney who teaches law at New York University.

Mr. Lewis, who left the State Department in 2017, said that in his experience, individual Saudi officers were often concerned or distressed by airstrikes that killed civilians but there was little institutional effort to reform the system.

The Joint Incidents Assessment Team, the body set up to investigate errant strikes, worked diligently at first, he said. But when its findings were made public, the Saudi Ministry of Foreign Affairs had removed any references that were critical of coalition actions.

Asked if that was the case, the Saudi ambassador to Yemen, Mohamed Al Jaber, said, "The JIAT is an independent team," and he referred any questions to them.

APPLYING LEVERAGE

Obfuscation and impunity continue to characterize the coalition's airstrike campaign. The coalition rarely identifies which country carries out an airstrike, although the vast majority are Saudi and Emirati, officials say. In July, King Salman of Saudi Arabia issued an order lifting "all military and disciplinary penalties" for Saudi troops fighting in Yemen, an apparent amnesty for possible war crimes.

Over the summer, as Emirati warplanes pounded the Red Sea port of Hudaydah, General Votel and the defense secretary at the time, Jim Mattis, held at least 10 phone calls or video conferences with Saudi and Emirati leaders, urging them to show restraint, a senior American military official and a senior Western official said.

At least one of the conferences involved Mohammed bin Zayed, the crown prince of Abu Dhabi and the effective leader of the United Arab Emirates.

"The Saudis are decent partners," Gen. C.Q. Brown Jr., a former top commander of American air forces in the Middle East, said in an interview. "And sometimes our partners don't always do things we would expect."

Short of halting all weapons sales, critics say the United States could pressure the Saudis by curtailing its assistance to the air war. Hundreds of American aviation mechanics and other specialists, working under Defense Department contracts, keep the Saudi F-15 fleet in the air. In 2017, Boeing signed a $480 million contract for service repairs to the fleet.

But after the departure of Mr. Mattis, who resigned last week, the Defense Department will be helmed by Patrick M. Shanahan, an arms industry insider. Mr. Shanahan, the acting defense secretary as of Jan 1., spent more than three decades at Boeing, the F-15 manufacturer which has earned further billions from lucrative service contracts in Saudi Arabia.

Pentagon officials said that in his current job as deputy defense secretary, Mr. Shanahan had recused himself from decisions involving Boeing.

Daniel L. Byman, a professor at Georgetown University's School of Foreign Service, said that a more robust policy toward Saudi airstrikes would not just be good for Yemeni civilians — it would also help the Saudis.

"This war has been a strategic disaster for the Saudis," he said. The airstrikes have shown no sign of defeating the Houthis, and the Houthis' foreign ally, Iran, has gained from Saudi Arabia's clumsy prosecution of the war.

"The United States needs to use its power to promote peace and stability in Yemen," Mr. Byman said. "And it needs to protect its allies from themselves."

DECLAN WALSH reported from Cairo, and ERIC SCHMITT from Washington.

Trump Administration
Steps Up Air War in Somalia

BY ERIC SCHMITT AND CHARLIE SAVAGE | MARCH 10, 2019

WASHINGTON — The American military has escalated a battle against
the Shabab, an extremist group affiliated with Al Qaeda, in Somalia even as President Trump seeks to scale back operations against
similar Islamist insurgencies elsewhere in the world, from Syria and
Afghanistan to West Africa.

A surge in American airstrikes over the last four months of 2018
pushed the annual death toll of suspected Shabab fighters in Somalia
to the third record high in three years. Last year, the strikes killed 326
people in 47 disclosed attacks, Defense Department data show.

And so far this year, the intensity is on a pace to eclipse the 2018
record. During January and February, the United States Africa Command reported killing 225 people in 24 strikes in Somalia. Double-digit
death tolls are becoming routine, including a bloody five-day stretch in
late February in which the military disclosed that it had killed 35, 20
and 26 people in three separate attacks.

Africa Command maintains that its death toll includes only
Shabab militants, even though the extremist group claims regularly
that civilians are also killed. The Times could not independently
verify the number of civilians killed. The rise in airstrikes has also
exacerbated a humanitarian crisis in the country, according to
United Nations agencies and nongovernmental organizations working in the region, as civilians are displaced by conflict and extreme
weather.

"People need to pay attention to the fact that there is this massive
war going on," said Brittany Brown, who worked on Somalia policy at
the National Security Council in the Obama and Trump administra-
tions and is now the chief of staff of the International Crisis Group, a
nonprofit organization focused on deadly conflicts.

The war in Somalia appears to be "on autopilot," she added, and one that is drawing the United States significantly deeper into an armed conflict without much public debate.

Somalia, a country that occupies a key strategic location in the Horn of Africa, has faced civil war, droughts and an influx of Islamist extremists over the years. The growing United States military engagement stands in stark contrast to the near-abandonment not long after the "Black Hawk Down" battle in 1993, which left 18 Americans and hundreds of militia fighters dead.

The intensifying bombing campaign undercuts the Trump administration's intended pivot to confront threats from great powers like China and Russia, and away from long counterinsurgency and counterterrorism campaigns that have been the Pentagon's focus since 2001.

Analysts suggested that the increase in American strikes may also reflect an unspoken effort by American commanders to inflict as much punishment on the Shabab while they can.

"Many of our commanders probably see a renewed urgency to degrade the enemy quickly and forcefully," said Luke Hartig, a former senior director for counterterrorism at the National Security Council during the Obama administration.

Gen. Thomas D. Waldhauser, the head of Africa Command, said planned cutbacks elsewhere would not affect what the military is doing in Somalia.

"We'll maintain our capability and capacity there," General Waldhauser told the House Armed Services Committee last Thursday. Africa Command is scaling back American forces nearly everywhere else on the continent in a move that poses a particular threat for West Africa, which is grappling with a range of extremist groups.

The Shabab formally pledged allegiance to Al Qaeda in 2012. But long before that, they fought Western-backed governments in Mogadishu as the group sought to impose its extremist interpretation of Islam across Somalia. In defending the fragile government, the United States has largely relied on proxy forces, including about 20,000

Gen. Thomas D. Waldhauser, the head of the military's Africa Command, testifying before Congress last Thursday. He said planned cutbacks elsewhere will not affect what the military is doing in Somalia.

African Union peacekeepers from Uganda, Kenya and other East African nations.

The United States estimates that the Shabab have about 5,000 to 7,000 fighters in Somalia, but the group's ranks are fluid. A State Department official, citing interviews from Shabab deserters, said that the number of hard-core ideologues may be as few as 500.

There are also now roughly 500 American troops in Somalia. Most are Special Operations forces stationed at a small number of bases spread across the country. Their missions include training and advising Somali army and counterterrorism troops and conducting kill-or-capture raids of their own.

The Shabab have proved resilient against the American airstrikes, and continue to carry out regular bombings in East Africa.

A range of current and former American officials said no seismic strategic shift explains the increased airstrikes and higher body count; the mission remains providing security so the fledgling Somali government will have time and space to develop its own effective military and security services.

But they noted a range of contributing factors for the rise in tempo and lethality of the military campaign.

Taking a page from counterinsurgency tactics developed in Afghanistan, American forces have helped Somali soldiers build several outposts across Somalia, about 20 percent of which is still controlled by the Shabab. One is named for Staff Sgt. Alexander W. Conrad, of Chandler, Ariz., who was killed in a mortar attack last year while he helped to build it.

The Shabab leadership views the outposts "as an irritant, masses to go after it, but fails," Maj. Gen. Gregg Olson, the Africa Command's director of operations, said in an interview.

In turn, that has put attacking Shabab fighters in the cross hairs of American airstrikes to defend the Somali forces.

Several officials said intelligence operations — including aerial surveillance, electronic intercepts and informant networks — have improved over the past year.

American troops with the secretive Joint Special Operations Command have built up informant networks that lead to raids and strikes, after which they collect cellphones, laptops and documents to generate information for more.

The drawdown of American military operations elsewhere in the world — including in Syria and, to a lesser immediate extent, Afghanistan — also has most likely freed up more drones and other gunships for use over Somalia, several former United States officials said.

"We were geared up for counterterrorism efforts in Somalia, and now there are more resources to do it, so we're doing more of it," suggested Stephen Schwartz, who served as the United States ambassador to Somalia from 2016 to 2017, although he cautioned that he had no current insider knowledge.

"It could be there is some well-thought-out strategy behind all of this," Mr. Schwartz added, "but I really doubt it."

The loosening of Obama-era constraints on using force in Somalia, as approved by President Trump in 2017, has also contributed.

Shortly after taking office, Mr. Trump declared Somalia to be an "area of active hostilities" subject to war-zone rules. That freed the United States military to carry out offensive operations whenever Shabab militants presented themselves — including against foot soldiers without special skills or roles.

Mr. Trump also delegated authority to commanders to carry out strikes without high-level interagency vetting. But Africa Command was initially slow to embrace it, waiting months before it carried out its first strike in 2017 under the new rules.

Now, however, it has opened the throttle, according to military data compiled by Bill Roggio, a senior fellow at the Foundation for the Defense of Democracies, who has tracked counterterrorism airstrikes for more than a decade on his Long War Journal.

Many of the recent airstrikes have targeted large groups of suspected fighters, killing more than 10 people in a single fierce swoop. Africa Command has disclosed strikes and estimated death tolls in a series of terse news releases, earning scant attention from Congress or the news media.

Along with the European Union and the United Nations, the United States also has continued to invest in so-called soft power assistance to Somalia, providing humanitarian aid such as food to drought victims, and development programs on education and training.

Officials cited signs of recent incremental progress in efforts to help the Somali government build a functional national army. And in December, the United States re-established a permanent diplomatic presence in Somalia for the first time since 1991. The current United States ambassador to Somalia, Donald Yamamoto, lives in Mogadishu, although the mission consists of a windowless bunker at the well-guarded airport.

There is good reason for caution. In 2013, Shabab militants carried out a deadly attack at the Westgate mall in the Kenyan capital of Nairobi. In January, they attacked a luxury hotel and office complex in Nairobi, killing 21 people. And in late February, the Shabab claimed a double bombing and the siege of a hotel in Mogadishu that killed at least 25 people.

General Olson said the military would continue to go after the Shabab as long as that is its mission.

"We go after the network when the network presents itself, whether a single node or a concentration," he said. "We've developed intelligence and are sussing out the relationship between the leadership and those being led; between those being led and those being trained or recruited or massed for an attack."

"We understand the network better than we have in years past," General Olson said.

THOMAS GIBBONS-NEFF contributed reporting.

The Secret Death Toll of America's Drones

EDITORIAL | BY THE NEW YORK TIMES | MARCH 30, 2019

President Trump is making it harder to know how many civilians the government kills by remote control.

THE PENTAGON SAYS American airstrikes in Somalia have killed no civilians since President Trump accelerated attacks against Shabab militants there two years ago.

Amnesty International investigated five of the more than 100 strikes carried out in Somalia since 2017 by drones and manned aircraft, and in just that small sampling found that at least 14 civilians were killed.

The Pentagon says airstrikes by the American-led coalition fighting the Islamic State killed at least 1,257 civilians in Iraq and Syria as of the end of January.

Airwars, a university-based monitoring group, estimates that those strikes killed at least 7,500 civilians in those countries.

Those disparities show how poorly the American public understands the human cost of an air war fought largely by remote-controlled drones. Drones have been the main weapon in the counterterrorism fight for more than a decade. They kill extremists without risking American lives, making combat seem antiseptic on the home front. But the number of civilians killed in these attacks is shrouded in secrecy.

President Trump has made it even harder to lift that shroud, by allowing the Central Intelligence Agency to keep secret how many civilians are killed in the agency's airstrikes outside of the Afghan, Iraqi and Syrian war zones — in places like Yemen, the lawless border region of Pakistan and North Africa.

President Barack Obama aggressively expanded drone use in these airstrikes. But he eventually came to understand the need for more transparency and accountability, and, under pressure, he put some sensible safeguards in place.

Among them was a July 2016 order requiring the government to issue annual public reports on the civilian death tolls in those areas.

Mr. Trump revoked that order this month. His National Security Council called it superfluous because Congress had subsequently passed a law mandating that the Pentagon publicly report any civilians killed in any of its operations. But that law covered only the Pentagon, not the separate C.I.A. drone campaign, which has broadened under Mr. Trump.

Experts say that, under President Trump, airstrikes have surged in Afghanistan, Iraq and Syria, as well as in Somalia. In Yemen, it is unclear to what extent the Americans, as opposed to the Saudi-Emirati coalition, are responsible. In Afghanistan, the number of American strikes that killed or injured civilians more than doubled in the first nine months of 2018 compared with the corresponding period in the previous year and killed more than 150 civilians, according to the United Nations Assistance Mission in Afghanistan.

Mr. Trump has also eroded constraints on civilian casualties.

Since taking office, he has rescinded rules that required the military and the C.I.A. operating outside of hot battlefields like Afghanistan and Iraq to limit their targets to high-level militants rather than foot soldiers. He also, by eliminating an elaborate interagency approval process, gave military commanders more authority to order drone strikes.

Yet, even under the previous rules, no matter how precise the weapons, how careful the planners and how skilled the fighters, mistakes, faulty intelligence, even calculated decisions often led to civilians being killed. The official data ranges from none to maddeningly vague, and the safeguards to mitigate civilian deaths are insufficient.

The military adopted an elaborate system under the Obama administration to minimize civilian casualties, including a requirement that forces have "near certainty" that no civilian will be harmed before launching an attack. But reporting by The Times and others in 2017 showed that the Pentagon had killed far more civilians in Iraq than it acknowledged.

The Obama administration estimated that over its two terms drone strikes had killed between 64 and 116 civilians in 542 airstrikes outside the major war zones. Micah Zenko, co-author of a new book, "Clear and Present Safety," calculated the real tally at roughly 324.

Drones, for all their faults, are less indiscriminate than B-52s or almost any other weapon. But they are also a seductive tool, potentially tempting presidents and military commanders to inflict grave damage without sufficient forethought.

A lack of transparency and accountability for civilian deaths helps enemies spin false narratives, makes it harder for allies to defend American actions and sets a bad example for other countries that are rapidly adding drones to their arsenals. It could also result in war crimes, as some critics have claimed.

Congress needs to insist on better data as the Pentagon inspector general investigates civilian casualty reporting.

There is no such thing as combat without risk. With drone combat, much of the risk falls on innocents. Americans need to understand the full cost and consequences of those risks.

CHAPTER 2

Measuring the Scale of Atrocity

In modern conflicts, determining facts on the ground can be a challenge. Even the number of casualties can be lost in the so-called "fog of war." When large-scale atrocities are suspected, understanding the process of fact-finding becomes especially critical. Aid workers, political actors, journalists and military operatives alike face different access barriers that limit knowledge of the situation. These articles reveal the simultaneously urgent and painstaking process of fact-finding, which combines cold numbers, political analysis and individual perspectives of the horror.

The Persecution of the Rohingya

EDITORIAL | BY THE NEW YORK TIMES | OCT. 29, 2014

THE GOVERNMENT OF MYANMAR has created a plan to expel the country's persecuted Rohingya Muslim minority. Under the proposal, all Rohingya who refuse to identify themselves as "Bengalis" (a term used for illegal migrants from Bangladesh) and do not have documentation acceptable to the government will be detained in camps before being driven out of the country. Incredibly, the government appealed to the United Nations last month for assistance with this project. The United Nations High Commissioner for Refugees, not surprisingly, refused to help relocate people being interned by their own government.

Some 140,000 of the estimated 1.1 million Rohingya in Myanmar are already living in internment camps, forced to flee their homes by anti-Muslim rampages incited by the radical Buddhist monk Ashin Wirathu and his extremist group 969. The conditions in the camps are appalling. In addition to malnutrition, a lack of medical care, employment and education, the Rohingya face beatings and torture by local authorities. More than 100,000 Rohingya have fled Myanmar by boat for Malaysia and Thailand. Thousands more have fled overland.

This is only the latest form of persecution. Under a 1982 law, Myanmar denied citizenship to the Rohingya, and last November it rejected a United Nations resolution calling for it to grant them citizenship. Instead, the government of President Thein Sein came up with the new proposal, which falsely holds out the possibility of citizenship at some future time, but only if the Rohingya agree to reclassification as Bengalis and have the required documents, which thousands of displaced people simply don't have. The plan would result in the enforced segregation and expulsion of a people based on their ethnic and religious identity.

Myanmar is expected to received $5 billion this fiscal year in foreign investments, thanks to the easing of economic sanctions by the United States and Europe on the promise of continued democratic and human-rights reforms. The United States and other governments must make it clear that Myanmar will face consequences if it continues to abuse the Rohingya.

Persecuted Yazidis Again Caught in Larger Struggle

BY THE NEW YORK TIMES | AUG. 11, 2014

THE YAZIDIS ARE a religious minority of about 500,000 people whose ancient monotheistic faith has roots in Zoroastrianism and beliefs involving a 12th-century mystic and a peacock angel. Those characteristics make adherents, who are neither Muslim nor Christian, apostates in the eyes of Islamist fighters who are sweeping through villages across northern Iraq.

Long stuck in the middle of an antagonistic relationship between Muslim Arabs and Muslim Kurds, the Yazidi people have been violently persecuted by both sides. After a particularly deadly crackdown in Iraq in 2007, the Yazidis were able to ensure a degree of security and influence through a carefully calculated alliance with the Kurds. Many Yazidis, who live in and around the region of northwestern Iraq known as Kurdistan, speak Kurdish, and some describe themselves as the original Kurds. The mostly Sunni Muslim Kurds say Yazidis are ethnic Kurds who simply follow a different religion.

In 2009, the Yazidis exploited Iraq's byzantine electoral rules to earn about a quarter of the seats in the government of Nineveh, one of the country's largest provinces, and became political allies with the Kurds in an Iraq that was becoming increasingly fractured along sectarian lines.

In recent days, as militants from the Islamic State in Iraq and Syria, or ISIS, have advanced in northern Iraq, driving religious minorities from their homes and killing others, the Yazidis have fled west of Mosul to Mount Sinjar, where they have been stranded for a week.

Their plight at the hands of Sunni fighters helped precipitate American airstrikes, authorized last week. The bombing of ISIS positions in the north appeared to alter the situation at Mount Sinjar. Four American airstrikes on the extremists surrounding the mountain on

The Bajid Kandal refugee camp operated by the United Nations in Dohuk Province.

Saturday, along with airdrops of food, water and supplies, have helped Yazidi and Kurdish fighters beat back ISIS and have enabled thousands of Yazidis to escape the militants' siege. The escapees made their way on Sunday through Syrian territory to Fishkhabour, an Iraqi border town under Kurdish control.

Tens of thousands more remain trapped on the mountain, and American officials cautioned that the limited airstrikes alone could not open a corridor to safety for them. Many families were separated, some in their flight to the mountains, some when they decided to descend.

Yazidis are now caught up in a larger disaster occurring across Iraq, but one that is hitting Iraqi Kurdistan, once the most stable part of the country, especially hard. Despite airdrops of aid from the Iraqi government and Americans, the humanitarian situation is worsening. Tens of thousands of Yazidis are trying to find refuge and relief in Kurdistan, near the borders with Syria and Turkey.

There, a mass migration, set off by increasingly widespread fears about the Sunni militants' advance, is underway. Christians fled Mosul earlier this summer as ISIS militants took over that city. And about 580,000 people displaced by fighting or the threat of violence have moved into the Kurdistan region, with about 200,000 having moved since last week when ISIS took Sinjar and its surrounding villages, according to David Swanson, a spokesman for the United Nations' Office for the Coordination of Humanitarian Affairs in Iraq.

ISIS Committed Genocide Against Yazidis in Syria and Iraq, U.N. Panel Says

BY NICK CUMMING-BRUCE | JUNE 16, 2016

GENEVA — Islamic State forces have committed genocide and other war crimes in a continuing effort to exterminate the Yazidi religious minority in Syria and Iraq, United Nations investigators said on Thursday, urging stronger international action to halt the killing and to prosecute the terrorist group.

The investigators detailed mass killings of Yazidi men and boys who refused to convert to Islam, saying they were shot in the head or their throats were slit, often in front of their families, littering road-sides with corpses. Dozens of mass graves have been uncovered in areas recaptured from Islamic State and are being investigated.

The investigators have produced 11 reports documenting wide-ranging crimes against humanity and war crimes committed by many parties to the five-year-old civil war in Syria, but in a report released on Thursday, they invoked the crime of genocide. They based their findings on actions taken by the Islamic State since August 2014 against 400,000 members of the Yazidi community, followers of a centuries-old religion drawing on many faiths.

"Genocide has occurred and is ongoing," Paulo Sérgio Pinheiro, chairman of the panel, the Independent International Commission of Inquiry on the Syrian Arab Republic, said in a statement.

"ISIS has subjected every Yazidi woman, child or man that it has captured to the most horrific atrocities," he told reporters in Geneva, using an acronym for the Islamic State. "ISIS permanently sought to erase the Yazidis through killing, sexual slavery, enslavement, tor-ture, inhuman and degrading treatment, and forcible transfer causing serious bodily and mental harm."

Those acts, he said, clearly demonstrated its intent to destroy the Yazidi community in whole or in part.

More than 3,200 Yazidi women were still being held by Islamic State fighters, mostly in Syria, the panel found.

"The crime of genocide must trigger much more assertive action at the political level, including at the Security Council," Mr. Pinheiro said, calling for the case to be referred to the International Criminal Court in The Hague, or to another international tribunal.

"Nothing has been done to save these people, and we hope for stronger action by the international community," Mr. Pinheiro said, highlighting the obligation for countries under the 1948 genocide convention to take action to prevent it.

The report compiled by the panel — based on interviews with survivors, religious leaders, smugglers and medical personnel, among others — had identified individuals responsible for acts of genocide and provided "a road map for prosecution," said Carla Del Ponte, a Swiss lawyer on the commission and a former prosecutor for the International Criminal Tribunal for the former Yugoslavia.

The commission on Syria has repeatedly recommended referral of the crimes to the International Criminal Court, but no action has followed from the Security Council, where Russia, a permanent member and the closest ally of Syria's president, Bashar al-Assad, wields a veto.

The commission had collected names and details of perpetrators and had shared information with some national authorities, said Vitit Muntarbhorn, a Thai legal scholar on the commission, who called the report "a wonderful gift" to the five permanent members of the Security Council "so that they can consider acting together."

Secretary of State John Kerry said in March that the United States had determined that Islamic State had committed genocide against Yazidis, Christians and Shiite Muslims, but Andrew Clapham, an international law professor at the Graduate Institute of International and Development Studies in Geneva, said the rigorous analysis presented by the commission of inquiry would carry more legal weight.

The Yazidis came to broad public attention after Islamic State fighters captured Mount Sinjar, in northern Iraq, in 2014 and engaged in systematic slaughter. Kurdish and Yazidi fighters retook Sinjar last fall.

Mass killings were only part of the Islamic State's systematic campaign to eliminate the Yazidi community, the panel found, citing documents that revealed careful planning for treatment of the community after it was overrun and a "massive organizational effort" to coordinate the actions of fighters across Iraq.

"ISIS made no secret of its intent to destroy the Yazidis of Sinjar, and that is one of the elements that allowed us to conclude their actions amount to genocide," Ms. Del Ponte said.

In addition to the killings, Islamic State fighters systematically separated Yazidi men and women and carried out rape, sexual mutilation and sterilization to prevent the birth of Yazidi babies, and they transferred captured Yazidi children to the fighters' families and training camps, cutting them off from Yazidi beliefs and practices and "erasing their identities as Yazidis."

The panel reported in harrowing detail the acute trauma experienced by women and girls as young as 9 who were sold off as spoils of war to become sex slaves of Islamic State fighters, routinely raped and punished with extreme violence if they resisted or tried to escape. Islamic State fighters often targeted younger Yazidi children as a means of punishing their mothers, the report said. It cited an account of a fighter who killed several children after their mother's effort to escape failed: The mother was then beaten and raped because she cried over their deaths.

"No other religious group present in ISIS-controlled areas of Syria and Iraq has been subjected to the destruction that the Yazidis have suffered," the report said.

As Atrocities Mount in Syria, Justice Seems Out of Reach

BY ANNE BARNARD, BEN HUBBARD AND IAN FISHER | APRIL 15, 2017

ISTANBUL — The evidence is staggering.

Three tons of captured Syrian government documents, providing a chilling and extensive catalog of the state's war crimes, are held by a single organization in Europe. A Syrian police photographer fled with pictures of more than 6,000 dead at the hands of the state, many of them tortured. The smartphone alone has broken war's barriers: Records of crimes are now so graphic, so immediate, so overwhelming.

Yet six years since the war began, this mountain of documentation — more perhaps than in any conflict before it — has brought little justice. The people behind the violence remain free, and there is no clear path to bring the bulk of the evidence before any court, anywhere.

More than 400,000 people have been killed in the Syrian war. Half the country's population has been displaced. Syrian human rights groups list more than 100,000 people as missing, either detained or killed. Tens of thousands languish in government custody, where torture, deprivation, filth and overcrowding are so severe that a United Nations commission said they amounted to "extermination," a crime against humanity.

But so far, only a handful of war-crimes investigations are being pursued by judicial authorities in Europe, and all the suspects in those cases are at large.

No cases have gone to the International Criminal Court. Syria never joined it, so the court's chief prosecutor cannot start an investigation on her own. The United Nations Security Council could refer a case to the court, but Russia has repeatedly used its veto power to shield Syria from international condemnation. And even if the Council were to take action, President Bashar al-Assad and his top officials are battened down in Damascus, making their arrests difficult, to say the least.

Destroyed buildings in Homs in 2014. More than 400,000 people have been killed in the Syrian war.

Earlier this month, the outside world was jolted by a chemical attack that killed more than 80 people. The United States government attributed the attack to Mr. Assad's forces based on flight data and other information. In response, President Trump let loose 59 Tomahawk missiles and called Mr. Assad an "animal."

As Mr. Assad has consolidated his control of Syria's major cities, some countries that have long opposed him have signaled a new willingness to accept his rule as the fastest way to end the war, encourage refugees to go home and accelerate the fight against the jihadists. As bad as Mr. Assad may be, some argue, Syria would be worse without him.

Mr. Assad's opponents counter that keeping a head of state with so much blood on his hands perpetuates the war.

The chemical attack was just his most recent atrocity, after years of torture, enforced disappearances, siege warfare and indiscriminate bombing of civilian neighborhoods and hospitals. The violence will continue as long as Mr. Assad and his security apparatus remain, his enemies say.

"This is not some abstract human rights issue," said Laila Alodaat, a Syrian human rights lawyer at the Women's International League for Peace and Freedom. "This lies at the core of this conflict and of any possible solution or reconciliation. Hundreds of thousands of victims and their families need justice, remedy and assurance that the future will be free from such violations."

Syria's war has seen atrocities by all sides. Rebels have shelled civilian neighborhoods, and the jihadists of Al Qaeda and the Islamic State have deployed suicide bombers, tortured enemies and executed prisoners, often on video.

But the largest number of violations by far has been by the Syrian government and its allies, investigators say, because they wield the apparatus of the state, including a formal military with an air force, extensive security services and networks of prisons.

The Syrian government portrays the conflict as an international conspiracy to destroy the country and equates all opposition with foreign-backed terrorism. It denies that its forces have used chemical weapons or committed atrocities.

In an interview last year, Mr. Assad said in response to a question from The New York Times that all prisoners are dealt with according to the law and dismissed the accounts of thousands of families who say their loved ones have disappeared without a trace.

"These are allegations," Mr. Assad said. "What are the facts?"

6 YEARS OF IMPUNITY

The Syrian uprising began with detention and torture in March 2011: A dozen boys were held after one of their friends wrote on a wall, "It's your turn, Doctor," suggesting that Mr. Assad, a former ophthalmologist, would be the next Arab leader to fall. They were arrested, beaten, tortured and forced to sign confessions, one told The Times.

As demonstrations spread, so did arrests. Syria already had a well-documented network of prisons where torture and forced confessions were common. But it expanded to what a United Nations Commission of Inquiry and human rights groups have described as an industrial scale, holding tens of thousands at any one time. Thousands have been executed in just one facility, Saydnaya prison, near Damascus, Amnesty International found.

The United Nations commission, in a report last year, quoted a defector from an intelligence agency as saying officers had orders to arrest male demonstrators between the ages of 16 and 40; another defector described his training in techniques that detainees have described, like beatings with cables, hanging by the wrists and electrocution.

Dozens of people over the years have told The Times in detail about their arrests and detentions and the disappearances of their relatives into the maw of the security system, from early 2011 to this month.

The arrests cut across political and socioeconomic lines. Yahya and Ma'an Sharbaji, two brothers, were arrested with a friend, Ghiath Matar, in September 2011, after leading protests in Daraya, a Damascus suburb. They had been part of a Muslim student group arrested years before for activities like holding discussions on liberalizing Islam and working for peaceful change. Mr. Matar's body was returned to his family with signs of torture; the Sharbaji brothers have not been seen since, according to the family.

In September 2012, Abdelaziz al-Khair, a leftist dissident, disappeared with his stepson Maher Tahan while leaving the Damascus airport, having flown in from abroad for an opposition conference.

His wife, Fadwa Mahmoud, has teamed up with Mr. Sharbaji's sister Bayan, and other women with missing family members, to fight for the rights of the detained and disappeared.

About 100,000 Syrians are still detained or missing, Ms. Mahmoud said in an interview, which affects perhaps a million family members. When men disappear, women, in a society with laws that privilege male authority, are left in limbo.

"They cannot grieve, they cannot remarry, they cannot sell property, the family has lost their breadwinner," she said.

It is rare to meet a Syrian refugee family that does not have a detained or disappeared member, and rarer still to find a former detainee who has not been tortured, said Sareta Ashraph, until recently the chief analyst for the United Nations commission.

K.K., a lawyer, was arrested in 2014, two years after he participated in a demonstration — with government permission — in Aleppo. He had also represented detainees, acidly commenting one too many times on a court system that finished trials in minutes and gave lawyers no access to their clients or the supposed evidence against them.

He described his eight-month ordeal in hours of interviews: daily beatings, a cell so packed that there was no room to lie down. He spent three months, he said, with personal space smaller than the size of a manhole.

In one of his first interrogations, he said, he was forced to count the blows, reaching 80 before he passed out.

Doused with cold water, he awoke to be hung for hours by his wrists, bound behind his back with handcuffs. Later, he saw a young detainee get doused with kerosene, and set on fire. It took him 20 days to die, untreated, of infection.

The torture went on until K.K. signed a confession of financing "terrorist" demonstrations — entirely fiction, he said, dictated by his captors.

Now K.K. works with other Syrian lawyers and former detainees to compile lists of victims, hoping their records will someday make a difference.

Other alleged war crimes take place in full view.

By 2013, bombings of rebel-held neighborhoods by artillery and warplanes had become routine. Hundreds of videos showed mutilated civilians, including women and children, pulled from rubble.

Hundreds of thousands of Syrians have lived under government siege, according to the United Nations, which has been repeatedly denied permission to deliver food and medical supplies. The chemical attacks of 2013, which killed more than 1,400 people in several Damascus suburbs, struck besieged areas like the town of Moadhamiyeh, making treating victims more difficult.

There have been dozens of cases of starvation, many of them children, and ill and elderly people.

The conflict has also seen what a recent paper by The Lancet and the American University of Beirut called "the weaponization of health care" — citing the arrest of doctors and systematic attacks on medical facilities. Nearly 800 medical personnel have been killed, more than 90 percent by the government, according to studies by Physicians for Human Rights.

In the days before the chemical attack this month, the main hospital in the area was hit by an airstrike. And a hospital several miles south was hit by another chemical attack — one of what medical groups working in opposition areas say have been dozens since Syria's government promised to give up its chemical weapons in 2014.

Since this month's chemical attack, residents have reported several attacks with incendiary weapons in Idlib and neighboring Hama provinces, uploading videos that show blinding fires typical of weapons like thermite and white phosphorus. They cause severe burns, similar to napalm, and their use is prohibited in civilian areas.

Many who have suffered lost hope of redress long ago.

A Syrian man who did four stints of detention and torture for taking humanitarian aid to wounded protesters and rebels recounted his experiences, but then expressed despair that anything would come of it.

"Countries don't need this evidence — they already know what's happening," said the man, Abu Ali al-Hamwi, using his nom de guerre because his mother is in government-controlled Syria.

"We are just pawns on a chessboard. I have women friends who were detained, raped, got pregnant, were tortured with acid."

He shrugged.

"There is no justice," he said. "And because there is no justice, there is no hope."

LIMITED STEPS TOWARD JUSTICE

As the war has dragged on, groups of activists, lawyers and others in Syria and beyond are documenting atrocities in hopes of one day bringing perpetrators to account.

Some film the aftermath of attacks and compile lists of the dead. Others are experienced war-crimes prosecutors who have begun building cases against Mr. Assad and other government officials.

The most systematic effort is by the Commission for International Justice and Accountability, a nonprofit group that has spent years taking captured government documents out of Syria.

The group, funded by Western governments, now has more than 750,000 Syrian government documents that contain hundreds of thousands of names, including those of top players in Syria's security apparatus, according to William H. Wiley, the group's executive director.

So far, the group has prepared eight detailed case briefs against ranking Syrian security and intelligence officials, Mr. Wiley said. Seven of them directly implicate Mr. Assad.

"Obviously, President Assad figures prominently in certain of the case files," Mr. Wiley said via Skype from his office in a European city that his organization keeps secret for fear of being targeted by the Syrian government. "Pretty much the entire military and intelligence security infrastructure of the regime is now featured in one or more of the prosecution briefs."

Strengthening these efforts are more than 50,000 images smuggled out of Syria in 2013 by a police photographer code-named Caesar, which show the dead and tortured bodies of thousands of detainees inside government security branches.

The photos have been verified by the Federal Bureau of Investigation and determined to contain images of 6,700 individuals, according to Stephen J. Rapp, who served as ambassador at large for war crimes during the Obama administration.

More than 700 of the people in the photos have been identified by name, opening other avenues for potential prosecution. Indeed, one of those photos led to the most recent legal action against Syrian officials.

In 2014, Amal Hag Hamdo Anfalis, a Spanish-Syrian hairdresser, received a text message from her niece containing a photo of a body she had seen on Facebook. She immediately recognized her brother, a truck driver who had disappeared at a Syrian government checkpoint a year earlier.

"As soon as I saw it, I completely collapsed and my children were wondering why I was crying," she said by phone from Madrid. "My children recognized him right away. They looked at the photo and said, 'That's our uncle.' "

The image was from the Caesar archive, parts of which activists had been posting online to identify victims.

Last month, a Spanish judge agreed to open an investigation into alleged state terrorism, accusing nine Syrian security and intelligence officials of using government institutions to commit mass crimes against civilians.

The defendants include Vice President Farouk al-Sharaa; Ali Mamlouk, head of the National Security Bureau; Gen. Jamil Hassan, head of air force intelligence; and senior officers at the prison where Ms. Hamdo believes her brother was detained and killed.

"To me, success in this case will be to keep it alive, to make these people's lives as complicated and miserable as possible," said Almudena Bernabeu, co-founder of Guernica 37 International Justice Chambers, which filed the case.

Judges and prosecutors in France and Germany are also investigating war-crimes allegations against Syrian officials for possible prosecution in domestic courts.

But even those working for war-crimes prosecutions face substantial barriers during a conflict.

The road to the International Criminal Court appears blocked, and European courts have trouble getting access to the accused. So the best-case scenario is often an international warrant that could lead to the suspects' arrests should they set foot in a country willing to cooperate.

Kevin Jon Heller, a law professor at SOAS at the University of London, said the evidence collected for Syria could be nearly as strong as that used in the Nuremberg trials after World War II.

"The problem as I see it is not so much what mechanism one can use to bring accountability, but how you actually get your hands on the people you want to prosecute," he said.

The limited prospects for prosecution have led some to pursue other kinds of justice.

"I don't think criminal prosecution alone is going to solve what has happened in my country," said Mohammad Al Abdallah, a two-time political prisoner who directs the Syria Justice and Accountability Center in Washington. "Institutional reform is more important than prosecution because it is what will have the longer-term impact on the country."

Alex Whiting, a Harvard law professor, said accountability is a matter of politics and so far Syria has not been high in the world's priorities. But he has been surprised, tenuously, since the latest chemical attack.

"Suddenly there is a turn in the world against Assad, which could lead to him being pushed from power, opening a space for accountability in the future," he said. "I'm not going to say it's likely, but it certainly seems more possible."

ANNE BARNARD reported from Istanbul; Beirut, Lebanon; Damascus, Syria; Geneva; and Düsseldorf, Germany; BEN HUBBARD from Beirut; and IAN FISHER from Jerusalem. Reporting was contributed by HWAIDA SAAD from Beirut, KARAM SHOUMALI from Istanbul, and SOMINI SENGUPTA from New York.

Myanmar's Rohingya Crisis Meets Reality

OPINION | BY KEVIN RUDD | SEPT. 21, 2017

THE NEWS COVERAGE of Myanmar over the past several months has led many people to conclude that Daw Aung San Suu Kyi, the de facto leader of the country, has abandoned her responsibility to protect human rights. Hundreds of thousands of people from the Rohingya ethnic minority are being expelled by the military from lands in western Myanmar, where they have lived for centuries. By any standard, we are witnessing the most fundamental violations of human rights.

Beneath these atrocities lie the complex internal politics of Myanmar. We need to remember what happened when, to international acclaim, Ms. Aung San Suu Kyi emerged as the democratic leader of Myanmar in November 2015, after nearly 50 years of military dictatorship.

The military denied her the title of president through a constitutional provision. And most important, following the transition from military rule to a form of democracy-lite, the military retained vast powers beyond its 25 percent stake in Parliament. It kept absolute authority over the country's defenses, internal security and border control — and over the entire Civil Service. That distribution of power has meant that Ms. Aung San Suu Kyi is legally prevented from directing the military or broader security forces to do anything against the wishes of the country's supreme military commanders.

This is the context for Ms. Aung San Suu Kyi's speech this week on the crisis in Rakhine State. Many people criticized her for not thundering against the military brutality in Rakhine, the home of most Rohingya. But the speech did strike a delicate balance between outright criticism of the military and the political constraints she faces.

She said that those guilty of human rights abuses will be dealt with under the full force of the law. Given that the military continues to hold power through the barrel of a gun, that position took courage.

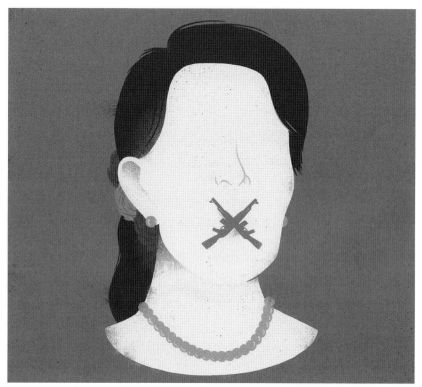

The military is not a monolith, and many hard-line generals would like to regain full control of the government. Ms. Aung San Suu Kyi's challenge has been to avoid providing the military with sufficient cause to justify a coup against her democratically elected government while also working toward long-term solutions for the Rohingya. The danger is that she falls between two stools — depicted by the military as too weak on "national security" while being seen in the eyes of the international community as too weak in her defense of an ethnic minority.

In her efforts to stabilize the situation in Rakhine, Ms. Aung San Suu Kyi appointed Kofi Annan, the former United Nations secretary general, to head a commission to make recommendations. The commission's final report, released in late August and fully embraced by

Ms. Aung San Suu Kyi, recommends, among other things, the closing of camps for internally displaced people, freedom of movement, minority participation in civic affairs and the creation of a mechanism to carry out the commission's recommendations.

But within days of the report's release, a newly insurgent terrorist organization, the Arakan Rohingya Salvation Army, attacked several border posts. The attacks were then used to justify the violent response from the military that led to the current appalling humanitarian crisis.

It is estimated that 200,000 to 400,000 people are being pushed toward Bangladesh. Some are making it across. Others are not. There are reports of rape, murder and entire villages being burned to the ground.

This is also affecting the people who live alongside the Rohingya Rakhine State. And the plight of all ethnic minority groups has been compounded by the deadly incursions of the Arakan Rohingya Salvation Army.

The military's campaign is part of a strategy to harness the Buddhist majority's deeply held sentiments against the Muslim Rohingya. But expelling the Rohingya also helps the military impugn Ms. Aung San Suu Kyi in the eyes of Myanmar's people. In pressuring her to voice some support for the plight of the Rohingya, the military is attempting to show that she is not prepared to stand up for the Buddhists against the Rohingya or other ethnic minorities deemed by popular sentiment to not be part of the Burmese nation.

The military also hopes to undermine Ms. Aung San Suu Kyi in the eyes of the international community, where she is seen as too weak in her defense of the Rohingya. The military has been succeeding in this, even though she has been largely powerless to act, given the legal, constitutional and realpolitik constraints she is facing.

The international community, therefore, faces a dual crisis of its own: First, an enormous humanitarian emergency in Rakhine State. Second, a military strategy manufactured to undermine Ms. Aung

San Suu Kyi's standing at home and abroad, and to pave the way for a return to a form of military rule.

When the United Nations sits down to decide what to do, both these factors must be considered.

The Rohingya must be protected as a matter of the highest priority. But so, too, must we stand up for the fledgling democracy in Myanmar. That requires not only demanding that the military end its brutal campaign against the Rohingya, but also not retreating from supporting Ms. Aung San Suu Kyi. And the body formed to carry out the Annan commission recommendations needs more international support.

Ms. Aung San Suu Kyi is no saint; no political leader is. Yet unless the international community focuses on the full dimensions of this crisis, not only will the humanitarian disaster for the Rohingya be prolonged, we will also see the end of democratic rule in Myanmar.

KEVIN RUDD, a former prime minister of Australia, is the president of the Asia Society Policy Institute.

How Syria's Death Toll Is Lost in the Fog of War

BY MEGAN SPECIA | APRIL 13, 2018

IN SEVEN YEARS, the casualties of Syria's civil war have grown from the first handful of protesters shot by government forces to hundreds of thousands of dead.

But as the war has dragged on, growing more diffuse and complex, many international monitoring groups have essentially stopped counting.

Even the United Nations, which released regular reports on the death toll during the first years of the war, gave its last estimate in 2016 — when it relied on 2014 data, in part — and said that it was virtually impossible to verify how many had died.

At that time, a United Nations official said 400,000 people had been killed.

But so many of the biggest moments of the war have happened since then. In the past two years, the government of President Bashar al-Assad, with Russia's help, laid siege to residential areas of Aleppo, once the country's second-largest city, and several other areas controlled by opposition groups, leveling entire neighborhoods. Last weekend, dozens of people died in a suspected chemical attack on a Damascus suburb, prompting the United States, Britain and France to launch retaliatory strikes against Syrian targets early Saturday.

In addition, American-led forces have bombed the Islamic State in large patches of eastern Syria, in strikes believed to have left thousands dead. And dozens of armed groups, including fighters backed by Iran, have continued to clash, creating a humanitarian catastrophe that the world is struggling to measure.

Historically, these numbers matter, experts say, because they can have a direct impact on policy, accountability and a global sense of urgency. The legacy of the Holocaust has become inextricably linked with the figure of six million Jews killed in Europe. The staggering death toll of the Rwandan genocide — one million Tutsis killed in 100 days — is seared into the framework of that nation's reconciliation process.

Without a clear tally of the deaths, advocates worry that the conflict will simply grind on indefinitely, without a concerted international effort to end it.

"We know from conflicts around the world that we can't have any sustainable peace if we don't have accountability," said Anna Nolan, director of The Syria Campaign, a human rights advocacy group. "The most critical thing to understand in that situation is who is being killed and who is doing that killing, and without that information we can't expect the people involved in resolving this conflict to come to the right decisions."

Until then, local monitoring groups keep the best estimates they can.

Fadel Abdul Ghany, the founder of the Syrian Network for Human Rights, said that there were "tens of incidents daily" that raise the death toll, and that monitoring was needed to one day hold perpetrators accountable for potential war crimes.

Despite the challenges of access and verification, he sees value in the assessment his group makes, even though he knows they are not perfect.

"This work, what we are doing, we are doing this mainly for our people, for our community, for history itself," Mr. Ghany said. "So we are recording these reports in order to say, on this day, in 2018, these people have been killed and because of this, and in this area."

He believes figures will be vital if peace comes to his country in establishing transitional justice.

"We don't want to lose any one life," he said.

The last comprehensive number widely accepted internationally — 470,000 dead — was issued by the Syrian Center for Policy Research in 2016. The group, which was based in Damascus until that year, was long seen as one of the most reliable local sources because it was not affiliated with the government or aligned with any opposition group.

But now, just getting a death certificate is problematic in Syria, let alone a collective tally of the dead, said Panos Moumtzis, a United Nations assistant secretary general and regional humanitarian coordinator for the Syrian conflict. And civilians make up the largest portion of the death toll.

Since there are 18 different authorities issuing documentation, in addition to the government in Syria, Mr. Moumtzis said, many civilians fear that having a death certificate issued by the "wrong authority" could jeopardize their relatives.

"Even in death, they worry that one day if they go to declare it they will be in trouble for it," Mr. Moumtzis said, further complicating tracking.

Some monitoring groups are still keeping count from afar, but their numbers vary, are estimates at best, and have not been verified by international groups. These monitors work with networks of contacts in Syria and collect reports on social media and from the news to compile casualty estimates.

The most prominent of these groups, the British-based Syrian Observatory for Human Rights, said last month that at least 511,000 people had been killed in the war since March 2011. Many organizations rely on this tally as the best current assessment. The group said in March that it had identified more than 350,000 of those killed by name; the remainder were cases in which it knew deaths had occurred but did not know the victims' names.

Another group, the Violations Documentation Center, which is linked to opposition groups, has a much lower estimate, tallying 188,026 conflict-related deaths from mid-March 2011 until March 2018. But the organization counts just civilian deaths and "takes a considerable amount of details before entering a name onto our database," Mona Zeineddine, a member of the group, said by email.

Mr. Ghany of the Syrian Network for Human Rights said he used tactics similar to those of the Syrian Observatory to track deaths, but his group counts only civilians. In late March, the network said 217,764 civilians had been killed since the beginning of the war.

The complexity of the conflict, the lack of direct access to conflict areas, and the ethnic and political divisions have made accurate counting an immensely challenging task, he said.

"In most of the incidents, we are unable to visit the places, and in Syria everyday we have tens of violations," Mr. Ghany said. "Each year has its own challenges and difficulties, and when you overcome one challenge, we face another."

Members of his group have been detained, and many now live outside Syria. The biggest challenge he now faces is apathy from those on the ground, as the protracted conflict continues.

"The people feel now that there is no hope and no need for all of this human rights work and this human rights documentation," Mr. Ghany said. "Because no one is listening to what we are doing."

Most international experts monitoring the conflict use a general figure of over 500,000 deaths, but acknowledge that changing conditions and restricted access make it impossible to know. Many believe it could be higher.

Based on that estimate, which takes into account both civilian and combatant deaths, around 2.33 percent of Syria's prewar population of 22 million has been killed.

At the start of the conflict, many journalists and diplomats had relied on the numbers from the Office of the United Nations High Commissioner for Human Rights, which worked with partners on the ground to tally figures. But the United Nations stopped officially counting in 2014, as the war intensified and became more complex.

"It was always a very difficult figure," a spokesman, Rupert Colville, said at the time. "It was always very close to the edge in terms of how much we could guarantee the source material was accurate."

In early 2016, the United Nations special envoy for Syria, Staffan de Mistura, said he believed an estimated 400,000 people had been killed. But Mr. de Mistura described it as an unrefined estimate based on earlier figures combined with recent reports of violence.

Now, most official communications from the United Nations simply cite "hundreds of thousands killed."

While the numbers vary, all of the groups agree on two things: that the Syrian government is responsible for the majority of the civilian deaths, and that calculating the toll is challenging.

"We often talk about these numbers, whether it's 400,000 or 500,000, but it's also about the trauma that is behind each of these numbers," said Mr. Moumtzis of the United Nations. "It has become almost mechanical, the number."

He added: "It's really just a cold figure, but behind it are lives."

Myanmar's Military Planned Rohingya Genocide, Rights Group Says

BY HANNAH BEECH | JULY 19, 2018

BANGKOK — Myanmar's military systematically planned a genocidal campaign to rid the country of Rohingya Muslims, according to a report released on Thursday by the advocacy group Fortify Rights based on testimony from 254 survivors, officials and workers over a 21-month period.

The 162-page report says that the exodus of around 700,000 Rohingya Muslims to Bangladesh last year — after a campaign of mass slaughter, rape and village burnings in Rakhine State in Myanmar — was the culmination of months of meticulous planning by the security forces.

Fortify Rights names 22 military and police officers who it says were directly responsible for the campaign and recommends that the United Nations Security Council refer them to the International Criminal Court.

"Genocide doesn't happen spontaneously," said Matthew F. Smith, a former Human Rights Watch specialist on Myanmar and China who is chief executive officer of Fortify Rights. "Impunity for these crimes will pave the path for more violations and attacks in the future."

Fortify Rights, a nonprofit organization registered in the United States and Switzerland, was formed in 2013 by Mr. Smith and fellow human rights activists. It has focused on investigating human rights abuses in Southeast Asia, particularly Myanmar.

Beginning in October 2016, Myanmar's military and local officials methodically removed sharp tools that could be used for self-defense by the Rohingya, destroyed fences around Rohingya homes to make military raids easier, armed and trained ethnic Rakhine Buddhists, and shut off the spigot of international aid for the impoverished Rohingya community, the Fortify Rights report says.

Most of all, more troops were sent to northern Rakhine State, where the bulk of the largely stateless Rohingya once lived. Fortify Rights says that at least 27 Myanmar Army battalions, with up to 11,000 soldiers, and at least three combat police battalions, with around 900 personnel, participated in the bloodletting that began in late August and continued for weeks afterward.

United States officials have said that the violence amounted to a calculated campaign of ethnic cleansing, and one United Nations official described the anti-Rohingya campaign as bearing "the hallmarks of genocide."

The Fortify Rights report suggests an alternate story line to the suggestion that the military-led atrocities, which were often abetted by ethnic Rakhine locals armed with swords, were solely a response to attacks by Rohingya militants on army and police posts on Aug. 25, 2017.

Myanmar's military and civilian government have consistently described the crackdown as "clearance operations" against Muslim "terrorists." Top military officers, including Senior Gen. Min Aung Hlaing, the army chief, have claimed that the military reacted with restraint following the deadly raids by the Arakan Rohingya Salvation Army in October 2016 and August 2017.

"There is no genocide and ethnic cleansing in Myanmar," said U Zaw Htay, a government spokesman. "Yes, there are human rights violations, and the government will take action against those who committed human rights violations."

Mr. Zaw Htay said that the Myanmar government would be forming an "investigation team, which will include internationally well-respected persons to investigate the human rights violations in Rakhine."

Several commissions, committees and investigative bodies have been formed in Myanmar to examine the Rakhine violence. But none have, so far, resulted in substantive shifts in policy or broad admissions of blame by the state.

Rohingya refugees waiting to board boats to Bangladesh on the bank of the Naf River in Myanmar last September.

"There are international organizations that accuse Myanmar with the terms 'genocide' and 'ethnic cleansing' without evidence," Mr. Zaw Htay added, naming Fortify Rights among them. "If there is evidence of genocide, then they can inform the government and our government will investigate and take action."

Fortify Rights has accused the international community of failing to adequately condemn the years of state repression of the Rohingya and, more specifically, the mounting abuses in the months preceding last year's military-led campaign.

The Fortify Rights report also describes how militants from the Arakan Rohingya Salvation Army killed and tortured Rohingya whom they considered to be government informants.

The list of Myanmar military officials whom Fortify Rights finds directly responsible for attacks on Rohingya Muslims include the commander in chief, Senior Gen. Min Aung Hlaing; his deputy,

Vice Senior Gen. Soe Win; and the chief of general staff, Gen. Mya Tun Oo.

Kerry Kennedy, president of Robert F. Kennedy Human Rights, a nonprofit advocacy group, just wrapped up a trip to Myanmar and Bangladesh, where she met with military and government officials, along with victims of the violence.

"What the United States should be doing," she said, "is to insist that the military and security forces that orchestrated this genocide are held accountable through targeted sanctions so this violence won't repeat itself."

When Myanmar was under full military rule, the United States and other Western governments placed sanctions on the army regime. But as the top brass began sharing power with a civilian government, most of those broad sanctions were lifted. Last December, Maj. Gen. Maung Maung Soe became the first Myanmar military officer subject to American sanctions because of his links to the ethnic cleansing of the Rohingya.

"We need more sanctions that target the people responsible for these abuses, like the over 20 officers that Fortify Rights names, to ban their travel, freeze their assets," Ms. Kennedy said. "What we don't want is sanctions that hurt the Myanmar population as a whole, which would harm the most vulnerable people."

SAW NANG contributed reporting from Mandalay, Myanmar.

383,000: Estimated Death Toll in South Sudan's War

BY MEGAN SPECIA | SEPT. 26, 2018

AN ESTIMATED 383,000 PEOPLE have died as a result of South Sudan's civil war, according to a new report that documents the extraordinary scale of devastation after five years of fighting in the world's youngest country.

The report, published by the London School of Hygiene and Tropical Medicine and financed by the State Department, revealed that about half of the dead were killed in fighting between ethnic rivals as it spread across the country, and the other half died from disease, hunger and other causes exacerbated by the conflict.

The number far surpasses earlier estimates from the United Nations and brings into focus the tragedy of a conflict that has received little global attention.

The researchers behind the report hope it will be instrumental in understanding the conflict and strengthening humanitarian responses.

"We hope that these kind of findings create even more urgency to actually making sure that the current peace deal is solid and is adhered to," said Francesco Checchi, the lead epidemiologist involved in the report.

UNDERSTANDING THE DEATH TOLL

While the numbers represent a stark increase from previous estimates, Mr. Checchi said the toll could well be higher.

The figure is the only comprehensive estimate of the death toll after nearly five years of war. There have been efforts to calculate the human cost on a community level over the years, with dozens of humanitarian groups conducting small-scale surveys.

The researchers whose report was released on Wednesday attempted to calculate the death toll from the beginning of the conflict in December 2013 until April 2018. Using population statistics and growth projections, and factoring in the intensity of the fighting, displacement, disease, access to health care and more, the epidemiologists produced a model that enabled them to estimate deaths month by month and county by county.

Assessments by humanitarian organizations and civic groups contributed to the projections.

The majority of the deaths occurred in the state of Central Equatoria, the country's bread basket, as well as in the northeastern states of Jonglei and Unity, all of which have been sites of major violence during the war. The death toll was highest in 2016 and 2017 after a power-sharing agreement brokered in 2015 fell apart.

Experts who have been monitoring the conflict for years say the new estimate offers a useful framework for understanding and responding to the war.

"For a long time, the absence of a death toll sanitized the horrors of the war and minimized its drastic effects," Brian Adeba, deputy director of policy at the Enough Project, a Washington-based group that monitors conflict in Africa, said in a statement. "This death toll reinforces the urgent need to hold accountable both the direct perpetrators and the leaders responsible for the violence."

WHAT ARE THE ROOTS OF THE CONFLICT?

South Sudan declared independence from Sudan in 2011, becoming the world's newest country, with the backing of Western nations. But two years later, civil war erupted in South Sudan.

The conflict began as a feud between forces loyal to President Salva Kiir and to then-Vice President Riek Machar. It soon spiraled into fighting among several factions, engulfing the country in ethnic violence and eventually producing a devastating humanitarian crisis.

Hunger and disease racked the country and millions fled to neighboring countries. Human rights abuses, mass rape and potential war crimes have been documented on both sides of the conflict.

WHY HAS IT BEEN SO HARD TO FIGURE OUT THE DEATH TOLL?

Because of violence, large portions of South Sudan have been inaccessible for periods of time. Aid workers have also been targeted during the conflict.

The Aid Worker Security Report, an annual global assessment of violence against aid workers, determined that last year, for the third year in a row, South Sudan was the most dangerous country in the world for aid workers. At least 113 aid workers have been killed in the country.

The epidemiologists who produced the new report had to find ways around the lack of access to many parts of South Sudan, Mr. Checchi said.

"Ordinarily what we might try to do in such a crisis scenario would be to carry out a large survey, take a sample nationwide and ask households to tell about their experience over the last few years, including deaths in their household," he said. "This was really not an option for South Sudan."

WHERE DOES THE CONFLICT STAND NOW?

On Sept. 12, a new peace agreement was signed by all parties to the conflict during a ceremony in Ethiopia. But the agreement does not address many of the issues at the core of the conflict, many experts say, and they fear it may not hold.

"With the peace agreement that was signed earlier this month being so structurally flawed, it is likely this number will continue its inexorable climb until the root causes of South Sudan's violence are addressed," John Prendergast, founding director of the Enough Project and co-founder of The Sentry, which researches the financing of conflicts, said in a statement.

The humanitarian crisis still needs to be confronted. Several nations met on the sidelines of the United Nations General Assembly in New York on Wednesday to discuss South Sudan.

Harriett Baldwin, a member of Britain's Parliament and the country's minister for Africa, called the latest peace accord a significant achievement, but said that it was "only the first step on a long journey to peace."

"Even since the most recent cease-fire, violence continues," she said.

Why Ilhan Omar and Elliott Abrams Tangled Over U.S. Foreign Policy

BY NIRAJ CHOKSHI AND MATTHEW HAAG | FEB. 14, 2019

IN A TENSE EXCHANGE at a hearing on Wednesday, one of the newest members of Congress, Representative Ilhan Omar, confronted Elliott Abrams, a Trump administration official, over his role in foreign policy scandals decades ago, including the Iran-contra affair and the United States' support of brutal leaders abroad.

Mr. Abrams, who served in top State Department positions under President Ronald Reagan and has remained part of the Washington foreign policy establishment, was appointed last month to be the Trump administration's envoy to Venezuela, where a dispute is raging over control of the nation's presidency. Last month, the United States weighed in, recognizing the opposition leader Juan Guaidó as part of a campaign by the Trump administration to oust President Nicolás Maduro.

WHAT HAPPENED AT WEDNESDAY'S HEARING?

Mr. Abrams was one of three people asked to appear before the House Foreign Affairs Committee for a hearing on Venezuela, an area of the world he knows well. Under Reagan, Mr. Abrams was an assistant secretary of state who fiercely advocated interventionism, including the covert arming of Nicaraguan rebels in the mid-1980s, a scandal that became known as the Iran-contra affair.

In the hearing on Wednesday, Ms. Omar, Democrat of Minnesota, confronted Mr. Abrams over his role in that scandal and his support for brutal Central American governments. In one tense exchange, Ms. Omar recalled testimony from Mr. Abrams about a massacre in which units of El Salvador's military, trained and equipped by the United States, killed nearly 1,000 civilians in 1981 in the village of El Mozote.

In 1982, Mr. Abrams dismissed news reports about the massacre as not credible and as leftist propaganda, and he later described the Reagan administration's record in El Salvador as a "fabulous achievement."

"Do you think that massacre was a 'fabulous achievement' that happened under our watch?" Ms. Omar asked him at Wednesday's hearing.

"That is a ridiculous question, and I will not respond to it," Mr. Abrams said. "I am not going to respond to that kind of personal attack, which is not a question."

WHAT IS THE IRAN-CONTRA AFFAIR?

The Iran-contra affair was a political scandal that dogged the second half of the Reagan presidency.

It centered on two controversial, and linked, actions undertaken by his administration. One was the sale of weapons to Iran, despite an embargo, purportedly to secure the release of American hostages held in Lebanon. The second was the use of proceeds from those weapon sales to support the right-wing contra rebels in Nicaragua in their fight against the leftist Sandinista government.

When first revealed publicly by a Lebanese magazine in 1986, the weapons sales were criticized for violating both the embargo and the United States' refusal to negotiate with terrorists. The use of money from the sales to support the rebels in Nicaragua was also controversial because it violated a congressional ban restricting military aid to the group.

Reagan emerged largely unscathed by the scandal, leaving office with the highest approval rating of any president in decades. But more than a dozen others were charged with criminal offenses, primarily for withholding information from Congress. They included some who remain active in American politics to this day, such as Oliver L. North, now the president of the National Rifle Association, and Mr. Abrams.

While serving in the State Department under Reagan, Mr. Abrams was a fierce advocate of arming the rebels and, in 1991, he pleaded guilty to two misdemeanor counts of withholding information from

Congress about those secret efforts. He was pardoned the next year by President George Bush.

WHAT WERE MS. OMAR'S CRITICISMS?

Ms. Omar devoted most of her time during the hearing to detailing Mr. Abrams's role in events abroad during the Reagan administration, often cutting off his responses by telling him she had not asked a question.

She did, however, ask one question: whether Mr. Abrams would "support an armed faction within Venezuela that engages in war crimes, crimes against humanity or genocide if you believed they were serving U.S. interests, as you did in Guatemala, El Salvador and Nicaragua?"

The United States' involvement in Guatemala is not as well known as the Iran-contra affair, but the country was crucial to the Reagan administration's strategy in Central America, with Washington often looking the other way when presented with evidence of atrocities. In 1982, the Reagan administration started to cultivate Gen. Efraín Ríos Montt, who seized power that year in Guatemala, as an ally in the region in its fight against the Sandinista government and Salvadoran guerrillas.

Reagan praised General Ríos Montt even though American officials privately knew the Guatemalan military had killed its own people. The general was convicted of genocide in 2013.

El Salvador officially apologized for the El Mozote massacre in 2011.

WHAT HAS MR. ABRAMS BEEN DOING SINCE THE REAGAN YEARS?

Despite his role in the Iran-contra affair, Mr. Abrams has remained active in politics.

In the 1990s, he led a think tank dedicated to applying Judeo-Christian values to public policy. He later joined the administration of President George W. Bush as an adviser on Middle East affairs.

In 2017, President Trump blocked Mr. Abrams from serving as a deputy to Rex W. Tillerson, then the secretary of state. But last month, Secretary of State Mike Pompeo was able to appoint Mr. Abrams as a special envoy to lead the department's efforts on Venezuela.

Rape and Torture as Weapons of War

While many features of war are devastating, rape and torture are uniquely world-destroying for the victims. They are also intentional acts that are often removed from the fighting. Torture is frequently used as a tool to terrorize the population, while rape is used as a "reward" to boost troop morale. The practice of both has been commonplace in war, either as an explicit policy or as a failure of military discipline. The articles in this chapter highlight the role that top-level policy can play in allowing rape and torture to persist.

U.N. Official Condemns Use of Torture in Syrian War

BY NICK CUMMING-BRUCE | APRIL 14, 2014

GENEVA — The United Nations human rights chief, Navi Pillay, condemned the rampant and routine use of torture by the Syrian authorities in a paper released by her office on Monday, which also records torture by some armed opposition groups and serious allegations of torture and the ill-treatment of children.

"Upon arrival at a detention facility, detainees are routinely beaten and humiliated for several hours by the guards in what has come to be known as the 'reception party,' " the report states, drawing on 38 interviews conducted by United Nations investigators over the last eight months with individuals released from detention centers across Syria.

"Our findings confirm that torture is being routinely used in government detention facilities in Syria, and that torture is also used by some armed groups," Ms. Pillay said. "In armed conflict, torture constitutes a war crime. When it is used in a systematic or widespread manner, which is almost certainly the case in Syria, it also amounts to a crime against humanity."

Among those interviewed, a 26-year-old woman detained for over two weeks described how security forces beat her and pulled out her teeth during interrogation sessions held every night and how, on one morning, she was tied up and raped by a security officer.

It also cites the account of a 60-year-old man who had spent three months in different detention centers and described how, every day, "cellmates were taken for 30 or 45 minutes of interrogation and came back with their faces bleeding, barely able to walk, and with open wounds that remained untreated and became infected."

Such cases were "illustrative of a much broader pattern of torture and ill-treatment," the paper noted.

"Men, women and children have been routinely picked up from the street, their homes and workplaces, or arrested at government-manned checkpoints," the paper said. Those detained came from all walks of life and had described being held in abhorrent conditions in cells crammed with prisoners and without sanitation, according to the report.

Investigators documented cases of people who had apparently died of torture, but whose corpses were delivered to their families in sealed coffins, preventing the identification of the cause of death. Sometimes the families received only identification papers of the deceased but not a body.

The United Nations paper said that torture by armed opposition groups was rare in the early stages of Syria's conflict, which began in March 2011, but that as of 2013, "this phenomenon appears to be on the rise." Investigators said they heard allegations that children perceived to be pro-government were tortured and treated poorly.

Two former detainees of the militant group Islamic State of Iraq and Syria cited in the paper described receiving severe beatings with electric cables, wooden sticks and rifle butts.

United Nations investigators said that several armed opposition groups, including the Islamic State of Iraq and Syria and the Nusra Front, had detention facilities in hospitals, schools and other public buildings in areas under their control, and that those most at risk of being held for interrogation included activists and people trying to document abuses.

In Syria on Monday, three journalists from Al Manar, Hezbollah's television station, were killed when gunmen fired on their car on the outskirts of the ancient Christian town of Maaloula, the station reported.

The Syrian Army seized control of Maaloula from rebels on Monday, and the reporters were among the journalists present to cover the events. Throughout the Syrian conflict, Al Manar has been sympathetic to President Bashar al-Assad, framing the conflict as a battle against extremists groups and terrorists.

BEN HUBBARD contributed reporting from Beirut, Lebanon.

ISIS Enshrines a Theology of Rape

BY RUKMINI CALLIMACHI | AUG. 13, 2015

Claiming the Quran's support, the Islamic State codifies sex slavery in conquered regions of Iraq and Syria and uses the practice as a recruiting tool.

QADIYA, IRAQ — In the moments before he raped the 12-year-old girl, the Islamic State fighter took the time to explain that what he was about to do was not a sin. Because the preteen girl practiced a religion other than Islam, the Quran not only gave him the right to rape her — it condoned and encouraged it, he insisted.

He bound her hands and gagged her. Then he knelt beside the bed and prostrated himself in prayer before getting on top of her.

When it was over, he knelt to pray again, bookending the rape with acts of religious devotion.

"I kept telling him it hurts — please stop," said the girl, whose body is so small an adult could circle her waist with two hands. "He told me that according to Islam he is allowed to rape an unbeliever. He said that by raping me, he is drawing closer to God," she said in an interview alongside her family in a refugee camp here, to which she escaped after 11 months of captivity.

The systematic rape of women and girls from the Yazidi religious minority has become deeply enmeshed in the organization and the radical theology of the Islamic State in the year since the group announced it was reviving slavery as an institution. Interviews with 21 women and girls who recently escaped the Islamic State, as well as an examination of the group's official communications, illuminate how the practice has been enshrined in the group's core tenets.

The trade in Yazidi women and girls has created a persistent infrastructure, with a network of warehouses where the victims are held, viewing rooms where they are inspected and marketed, and a dedicated fleet of buses used to transport them.

A 12-year-old girl in the Kurdistan region of northern Iraq.

A total of 5,270 Yazidis were abducted last year, and at least 3,144 are still being held, according to community leaders. To handle them, the Islamic State has developed a detailed bureaucracy of sex slavery, including sales contracts notarized by the ISIS-run Islamic courts. And the practice has become an established recruiting tool to lure men from deeply conservative Muslim societies, where casual sex is taboo and dating is forbidden.

A growing body of internal policy memos and theological discussions has established guidelines for slavery, including a lengthy how-to manual issued by the Islamic State Research and Fatwa Department just last month. Repeatedly, the ISIS leadership has emphasized a narrow and selective reading of the Quran and other religious rulings to not only justify violence, but also to elevate and celebrate each sexual assault as spiritually beneficial, even virtuous.

"Every time that he came to rape me, he would pray," said F, a 15-year-old girl who was captured on the shoulder of Mount Sinjar one year ago and was sold to an Iraqi fighter in his 20s. Like some others interviewed by The New York Times, she wanted to be identified only by her first initial because of the shame associated with rape.

"He kept telling me this is ibadah," she said, using a term from Islamic scripture meaning worship.

"He said that raping me is his prayer to God. I said to him, 'What you're doing to me is wrong, and it will not bring you closer to God.' And he said, 'No, it's allowed. It's halal,' " said the teenager, who escaped in April with the help of smugglers after being enslaved for nearly nine months.

CALCULATED CONQUEST

The Islamic State's formal introduction of systematic sexual slavery dates to Aug. 3, 2014, when its fighters invaded the villages on the southern flank of Mount Sinjar, a craggy massif of dun-colored rock in northern Iraq.

Its valleys and ravines are home to the Yazidis, a tiny religious minority who represent less than 1.5 percent of Iraq's estimated population of 34 million.

The offensive on the mountain came just two months after the fall of Mosul, the second-largest city in Iraq. At first, it appeared that the subsequent advance on the mountain was just another attempt to extend the territory controlled by Islamic State fighters.

Almost immediately, there were signs that their aim this time was different.

Survivors say that men and women were separated within the first hour of their capture. Adolescent boys were told to lift up their shirts, and if they had armpit hair, they were directed to join their older brothers and fathers. In village after village, the men and older boys were driven or marched to nearby fields, where they were forced to lie down in the dirt and sprayed with automatic fire.

The women, girls and children, however, were hauled off in open-bed trucks.

A 15-year-old girl who wished to be identified only as F, right, with her father and 4-year-old brother. "Every time that he came to rape me, he would pray," said F, who was captured by the Islamic State on Mount Sinjar one year ago and sold to an Iraqi fighter.

"The offensive on the mountain was as much a sexual conquest as it was for territorial gain," said Matthew Barber, a University of Chicago expert on the Yazidi minority. He was in Dohuk, near Mount Sinjar, when the onslaught began last summer and helped create a foundation that provides psychological support for the escapees, who number more than 2,000, according to community activists.

Fifteen-year-old F says her family of nine was trying to escape, speeding up mountain switchbacks, when their aging Opel overheated. She, her mother, and her sisters — 14, 7, and 4 years old — were helplessly standing by their stalled car when a convoy of heavily armed Islamic State fighters encircled them.

"Right away, the fighters separated the men from the women," she said. She, her mother and sisters were first taken in trucks to the nearest town on Mount Sinjar. "There, they separated me from my mom. The young, unmarried girls were forced to get into buses."

The buses were white, with a painted stripe next to the word "Hajj," suggesting that the Islamic State had commandeered Iraqi government buses used to transport pilgrims for the annual pilgrimage to Mecca. So many Yazidi women and girls were loaded inside F's bus that they were forced to sit on each other's laps, she said.

Once the bus headed out, they noticed that the windows were blocked with curtains, an accoutrement that appeared to have been added because the fighters planned to transport large numbers of women who were not covered in burqas or head scarves.

F's account, including the physical description of the bus, the placement of the curtains and the manner in which the women were transported, is echoed by a dozen other female victims interviewed for this article. They described a similar set of circumstances even though they were kidnapped on different days and in locations miles apart.

F says she was driven to the Iraqi city of Mosul some six hours away, where they herded them into the Galaxy Wedding Hall. Other groups of women and girls were taken to a palace from the Saddam Hussein era, the Badoosh prison compound and the Directory of Youth building in Mosul, recent escapees said. And in addition to Mosul, women were herded into elementary schools and municipal buildings in the Iraqi towns of Tal Afar, Solah, Ba'aj and Sinjar City.

They would be held in confinement, some for days, some for months. Then, inevitably, they were loaded into the same fleet of buses again before being sent in smaller groups to Syria or to other locations inside Iraq, where they were bought and sold for sex.

"It was 100 percent preplanned," said Khider Domle, a Yazidi community activist who maintains a detailed database of the victims. "I spoke by telephone to the first family who arrived at the Directory of Youth in Mosul, and the hall was already prepared for them. They had mattresses, plates and utensils, food and water for hundreds of people."

Detailed reports by Human Rights Watch and Amnesty International reach the same conclusion about the organized nature of the sex trade.

In each location, survivors say Islamic State fighters first conducted a census of their female captives.

Inside the voluminous Galaxy banquet hall, F sat on the marble floor, squeezed between other adolescent girls. In all she estimates there were over 1,300 Yazidi girls sitting, crouching, splayed out and leaning against the walls of the ballroom, a number that is confirmed by several other women held in the same location.

They each described how three Islamic State fighters walked in, holding a register. They told the girls to stand. Each one was instructed to state her first, middle and last name, her age, her hometown, whether she was married, and if she had children.

For two months, F was held inside the Galaxy hall. Then one day, they came and began removing young women. Those who refused were dragged out by their hair, she said.

In the parking lot the same fleet of Hajj buses was waiting to take them to their next destination, said F. Along with 24 other girls and young women, the 15-year-old was driven to an army base in Iraq. It was there in the parking lot that she heard the word "sabaya" for the first time.

"They laughed and jeered at us, saying 'You are our sabaya.' I didn't know what that word meant," she said. Later on, the local Islamic State leader explained it meant slave.

"He told us that Taus Malik" — one of seven angels to whom the Yazidis pray — "is not God. He said that Taus Malik is the devil and that because you worship the devil, you belong to us. We can sell you and use you as we see fit."

The Islamic State's sex trade appears to be based solely on enslaving women and girls from the Yazidi minority. As yet, there has been no widespread campaign aimed at enslaving women from other religious minorities, said Samer Muscati, the author of the recent Human Rights Watch report. That assertion was echoed by community leaders, government officials and other human rights workers.

Mr. Barber, of the University of Chicago, said that the focus on Yazidis was likely because they are seen as polytheists, with an oral tradition rather than a written scripture. In the Islamic State's eyes that puts them on the fringe of despised unbelievers, even more than Christians and Jews, who are considered to have some limited protections under the Quran as "People of the Book."

In Kojo, one of the southernmost villages on Mount Sinjar and among the farthest away from escape, residents decided to stay, believing they would be treated as the Christians of Mosul had months earlier. On Aug. 15, 2014, the Islamic State ordered the residents to report to a school in the center of town.

When she got there, 40-year-old Aishan Ali Saleh found a community elder negotiating with the Islamic State, asking if they could be allowed to hand over their money and gold in return for safe passage.

The fighters initially agreed and laid out a blanket, where Ms. Saleh placed her heart-shaped pendant and her gold rings, while the men left crumpled bills.

Instead of letting them go, the fighters began shoving the men outside, bound for death.

Sometime later, a fleet of cars arrived and the women, girls and children were driven away.

THE MARKET

Months later, the Islamic State made clear in its online magazine that its campaign of enslaving Yazidi women and girls had been extensively preplanned.

"Prior to the taking of Sinjar, Shariah students in the Islamic State were tasked to research the Yazidis," said the English-language article, headlined "The Revival of Slavery Before the Hour," which appeared in the October issue of the magazine, Dabiq.

The article made clear that for the Yazidis, there was no chance to pay a tax known as jizya to be set free, "unlike the Jews and Christians."

"After capture, the Yazidi women and children were then divided according to the Shariah amongst the fighters of the Islamic State who participated in the Sinjar operations, after one fifth of the slaves were transferred to the Islamic State's authority to be divided" as spoils, the article said.

In much the same way as specific Bible passages were used centuries later to support the slave trade in the United States, the Islamic State cites specific verses or stories in the Quran or else in the Sunna, the traditions based on the sayings and deeds of the Prophet Muhammad, to justify their human trafficking, experts say.

Scholars of Islamic theology disagree, however, on the proper interpretation of these verses, and on the divisive question of whether Islam actually sanctions slavery.

Many argue that slavery figures in Islamic scripture in much the same way that it figures in the Bible — as a reflection of the period in antiquity in which the religion was born.

"In the milieu in which the Quran arose, there was a widespread practice of men having sexual relationships with unfree women," said Kecia Ali, an associate professor of religion at Boston University and the author of a book on slavery in early Islam. "It wasn't a particular religious institution. It was just how people did things."

Cole Bunzel, a scholar of Islamic theology at Princeton University, disagrees, pointing to the numerous references to the phrase "Those your right hand possesses" in the Quran, which for centuries has been interpreted to mean female slaves. He also points to the corpus of Islamic jurisprudence, which continues into the modern era and which he says includes detailed rules for the treatment of slaves.

"There is a great deal of scripture that sanctions slavery," said Mr. Bunzel, the author of a research paper published by the Brookings Institution on the ideology of the Islamic State. "You can argue that it is no longer relevant and has fallen into abeyance. ISIS would argue that these institutions need to be revived, because that is what the Prophet and his companions did."

The youngest, prettiest women and girls were bought in the first weeks after their capture. Others — especially older, married women — described how they were transported from location to location, spending months in the equivalent of human holding pens, until a prospective buyer bid on them.

Their captors appeared to have a system in place, replete with its own methodology of inventorying the women, as well as their own lexicon. Women and girls were referred to as "Sabaya," followed by their name. Some were bought by wholesalers, who photographed and gave them numbers, to advertise them to potential buyers.

Osman Hassan Ali, a Yazidi businessman who has successfully smuggled out numerous Yazidi women, said he posed as a buyer in order to be sent the photographs. He shared a dozen images, each one showing a Yazidi woman sitting in a bare room on a couch, facing the camera with a blank, unsmiling expression. On the edge of the photograph is written in Arabic, "Sabaya No. 1," "Sabaya No. 2," and so on.

Buildings where the women were collected and held sometimes included a viewing room.

"When they put us in the building, they said we had arrived at the 'Sabaya Market,'" said one 19-year-old victim, whose first initial is I. "I understood we were now in a slave market."

She estimated there were at least 500 other unmarried women and girls in the multistory building, with the youngest among them being 11. When the buyers arrived, the girls were taken one by one into a separate room.

"The emirs sat against the wall and called us by name. We had to sit in a chair facing them. You had to look at them, and before you went in, they took away our scarves and anything we could have used to cover ourselves," she said.

"When it was my turn, they made me stand four times. They made me turn around."

The captives were also forced to answer intimate questions, including reporting the exact date of their last menstrual cycle. They realized that the fighters were trying to determine whether they were pregnant, in keeping with a Shariah rule stating that a man cannot have intercourse with his slave if she is pregnant.

The use of sex slavery by the Islamic State initially surprised even the group's most ardent supporters, many of whom sparred with journalists online after the first reports of systematic rape.

The Islamic State's leadership has repeatedly sought to justify the practice to its internal audience.

After the initial article in Dabiq in October, the issue came up in the publication again this year, in an editorial in May that expressed the writer's hurt and dismay at the fact that some of the group's own sympathizers had questioned the institution of slavery.

"What really alarmed me was that some of the Islamic State's supporters started denying the matter as if the soldiers of the Khilafah had committed a mistake or evil," the author wrote. "I write this while the letters drip of pride," she said. "We have indeed raided and captured the kafirah women and drove them like sheep by the edge of the sword." Kafirah refers to infidels.

In a pamphlet published online in December, the Research and Fatwa Department of the Islamic State detailed best practices, including explaining that slaves belong to the estate of the fighter who bought them and therefore can be willed to another man and disposed of just like any other property after his death.

Recent escapees describe an intricate bureaucracy surrounding their captivity, with their status as a slave registered in a contract. When their owner would sell them to another buyer, a new contract would be drafted, like transferring a property deed. At the same time, slaves can also be set free, and fighters are promised a heavenly reward for doing so.

Though rare, this has created one avenue of escape for victims.

A 25-year-old victim who escaped last month, identified by her first initial, A, described how one day her Libyan master handed her a laminated piece of paper. He explained that he had finished his training as a suicide bomber and was planning to blow himself up, and was therefore setting her free.

A woman, who said she was raped by Islamic State militants, at a refugee camp in the Kurdistan region of northern Iraq.

Labeled a "Certificate of Emancipation," the document was signed by the judge of the western province of the Islamic State. The Yazidi woman presented it at security checkpoints as she left Syria to return to Iraq, where she rejoined her family in July.

The Islamic State recently made it clear that sex with Christian and Jewish women captured in battle is also permissible, according to a new 34-page manual issued this summer by the terror group's Research and Fatwa Department.

Just about the only prohibition is having sex with a pregnant slave, and the manual describes how an owner must wait for a female captive to have her menstruating cycle, in order to "make sure there is nothing in her womb," before having intercourse with her. Of the 21 women and girls interviewed for this article, among the only ones who had not been raped were the women who were already pregnant at the moment of their capture, as well as those who were past menopause.

Beyond that, there appears to be no bounds to what is sexually permissible. Child rape is explicitly condoned: "It is permissible to have intercourse with the female slave who hasn't reached puberty, if she is fit for intercourse," according to a translation by the Middle East Media Research Institute of a pamphlet published on Twitter last December.

One 34-year-old Yazidi woman, who was bought and repeatedly raped by a Saudi fighter in the Syrian city of Shadadi, described how she fared better than the second slave in the household — a 12-year-old girl who was raped for days on end despite heavy bleeding.

"He destroyed her body. She was badly infected. The fighter kept coming and asking me, 'Why does she smell so bad?' And I said, she has an infection on the inside, you need to take care of her," the woman said.

Unmoved, he ignored the girl's agony, continuing the ritual of praying before and after raping the child.

"I said to him, 'She's just a little girl,' " the older woman recalled. "And he answered: 'No. She's not a little girl. She's a slave. And she knows exactly how to have sex.' "

"And having sex with her pleases God," he said.

How to Counter Rape During War

OPINION | BY ELISABETH JEAN WOOD AND DARA KAY COHEN | OCT. 28, 2015

LAST YEAR, AT a global conference on sexual violence during war, many speakers agreed that the best way to deter such crimes was prosecution, and they called for more of it. But prosecutions are not enough. We must work to reduce sexual violence by armed groups *during* wars — not just act afterward.

First, we have to better understand it. Although rape during war is an ancient crime, it's only in the last decade that social scientists have begun to study the patterns in which soldiers and rebels rape. The findings may be surprising: It's not more likely to occur in particular regions, countries with greater gender inequality or during ethnic conflict; men may be victims, and women can be perpetrators.

But while rape is tragically common in war zones, it's not an inevitable part of war. In fact, we have found that a significant percentage of both armies and rebel groups in recent civil wars were, surprisingly, not reported to have raped civilians. That's because commanders have options: They can choose to order, tolerate or prohibit rape. A deeper understanding of their behavior offers the hope of mitigating the problem.

Some commanders order rape as a military or political strategy, and specify the target. As the Soviet Army marched toward Germany in 1945, generals ordered soldiers to take revenge on all Germans, not just soldiers. Guatemalan soldiers systematically raped indigenous Mayans during the civil war from 1960 to 1996. Today, the Islamic State forces Yazidi women and girls into marriages and sexual slavery, which they wrongly believe is legitimate under Islamic law.

Other commanders, even when they don't order rape, implicitly or explicitly tolerate it. And rape can become extremely widespread, although it's not ordered. In these cases, we have found that the motivation to rape often comes from soldiers' interactions with one another.

It may reflect soldiers' frustration in fighting an enemy that is difficult to engage, as it was for those units of American troops who raped
Vietnamese civilians in the 1960s. It can also be a form of self-pay, as
it is for Congolese soldiers who say that they rape out of anger that
their meager salary prevents them from achieving masculine ideals,
like providing for a family. Gang rape, in particular, may allow soldiers
who were conscripted by force to create bonds of friendship and loy-
alty, as male and female members of the Revolutionary United Front
in Sierra Leone reported.

Finally, some commanders prohibit rape by their soldiers. In Sri
Lanka the Tamil Tigers, while otherwise very violent during their
insurgency in the 1980s and '90s, closely monitored their troops and
brutally punished the few soldiers who raped. In El Salvador in the
1980s, commanders of the Farabundo Martí National Liberation
Front required their fighters to attend classes that emphasized that
the group's Marxist ideology prohibited the abuse of civilians. Rape
was already infrequent, but after classes started, it virtually ended.
Although both the Israel Defense Forces and Palestinian militant
groups commit other acts of violence, rape has been extremely rare
in recent years.

Unlike a stray bullet, rape is always intentional — whether it's
ordered from above or emerges from below. That simple fact means
there is a lot that military officers and leaders of insurgent groups,
NGOs and government agencies can do to mitigate it.

To counter rape during war, the international community has
focused heavily on increasing prosecutions. Prosecutions are important because they confirm to survivors that rape is a crime and an
injustice. But prosecutors often seek evidence of an explicit policy.
This leaves out commanders who tolerate rape, even if they don't order
it. They, too, should be held responsible.

Moreover, prosecutions are insufficient. Trials are too costly, slow
and small in scope. And there is little evidence to suggest they have a
deterrent effect.

Instead, we should work to prevent rape during conflicts. To do so, we must understand specific traits of armed groups — their ideology, morals and laws, as well as how commanders recruit, discipline and pay soldiers — which can help predict whether a group might rape, and how.

Scholars have found that organizations that recruit by kidnapping are significantly more likely to perpetrate widespread gang rape than those that don't. Groups that torture detainees are more likely to engage in sexual violence as well. These characteristics, if better understood, could serve as early warning signs for those who want to prevent rape from happening or worsening once it starts.

For instance, armies that rape should be publicly named and shamed, a tactic that research shows significantly ameliorated the severity of genocides and state-sponsored killing in the last several decades. If a soldier is widely identified as a rapist, or a commander is known around the world to tolerate rape, the shame and threat to their reputation may dissuade their peers — particularly those who seek international legitimacy — from raping.

Countries should make aid and weapon transfers to armed groups conditional on their human rights record and swiftly withdraw both if soldiers are reported to rape civilians. And they must punish leaders of armed groups who order or tolerate rape by imposing targeted sanctions, like travel bans and asset freezes. These options may convince leaders of armed groups that the cost of rape is too high.

Such tactics won't work with groups like the Islamic State that reject international law and do not rely on external funding. Instead, the testimonies of recruits who have defected could become powerful deterrents if they are widely publicized.

Moreover, many Muslim scholars around the world have rejected the Islamic State's interpretation of their faith. Some prominent jihadists have even called it "deviant." These figures have the credibility that Western policy makers lack to critique the Islamic State's ideology.

Thanks to the courageous work of lawyers and activists, rape is no longer "the greatest silence." Many survivors around the world report it, despite the significant risks. The challenge today is not to make an invisible crime more visible. It is to apply what has been learned over the past decades to prevent it.

ELISABETH JEAN WOOD, a professor of political science at Yale, is the author of the forthcoming book "Sexual Violence During War." **DARA KAY COHEN**, an assistant professor of public policy at Harvard, is the author of the forthcoming book "Rape During Civil War."

How U.S. Torture Left a Legacy of Damaged Minds

BY MATT APUZZO, SHERI FINK AND JAMES RISEN | OCT. 8, 2016

Beatings, sleep deprivation, menacing and other brutal tactics have led to persistent mental health problems among detainees held in secret C.I.A. prisons and at Guantánamo.

BEFORE THE UNITED STATES permitted a terrifying way of interrogating prisoners, government lawyers and intelligence officials assured themselves of one crucial outcome. They knew that the methods inflicted on terrorism suspects would be painful, shocking and far beyond what the country had ever accepted. But none of it, they concluded, would cause long lasting psychological harm.

Fifteen years later, it is clear they were wrong.

Today in Slovakia, Hussein al-Marfadi describes permanent headaches and disturbed sleep, plagued by memories of dogs inside a blackened jail. In Kazakhstan, Lutfi bin Ali is haunted by nightmares of suffocating at the bottom of a well. In Libya, the radio from a passing car spurs rage in Majid Mokhtar Sasy al-Maghrebi, reminding him of the C.I.A. prison where earsplitting music was just one assault to his senses.

And then there is the despair of men who say they are no longer themselves. "I am living this kind of depression," said Younous Chekkouri, a Moroccan, who fears going outside because he sees faces in crowds as Guantánamo Bay guards. "I'm not normal anymore."

After enduring agonizing treatment in secret C.I.A. prisons around the world or coercive practices at the military detention camp at Guantánamo Bay, Cuba, dozens of detainees developed persistent mental health problems, according to previously undisclosed medical records, government documents and interviews with former prisoners and military and civilian doctors. Some emerged with the same symptoms as American prisoners of war who were brutalized decades earlier by some of the world's cruelest regimes.

Lutfi bin Ali, a former detainee now living in Kazakhstan, has chronic health problems and undergoes physical therapy for injuries he sustained in custody.

Those subjected to the tactics included victims of mistaken identity or flimsy evidence that the United States later disavowed. Others were foot soldiers for the Taliban or Al Qaeda who were later deemed to pose little threat. Some were hardened terrorists, including those accused of plotting the Sept. 11 attacks or the 2000 bombing of the American destroyer Cole. In several cases, their mental status has complicated the nation's long effort to bring them to justice.

Americans have long debated the legacy of post-Sept. 11 interrogation methods, asking whether they amounted to torture or succeeded in extracting intelligence. But even as President Obama continues transferring people from Guantánamo and Donald J. Trump, the Republican presidential nominee, promises to bring back techniques, now banned, such as waterboarding, the human toll has gone largely uncalculated.

At least half of the 39 people who went through the C.I.A.'s "enhanced interrogation" program, which included depriving them of sleep, dousing them with ice water, slamming them into walls and locking them in coffin-like boxes, have since shown psychiatric problems, The New York Times found. Some have been diagnosed with post-traumatic stress disorder, paranoia, depression or psychosis.

Hundreds more detainees moved through C.I.A. "black sites" or Guantánamo, where the military inflicted sensory deprivation, isolation, menacing with dogs and other tactics on men who now show serious damage. Nearly all have been released.

"There is no question that these tactics were entirely inconsistent with our values as Americans, and their consequences present lasting challenges for us as a country and for the individuals involved," said Ben Rhodes, the deputy national security adviser.

The United States government has never studied the long-term psychological effects of the extraordinary interrogation practices it embraced. A Defense Department spokeswoman, asked about long-term mental harm, responded that prisoners were treated humanely and had access to excellent care. A C.I.A. spokesman declined to comment.

This article is based on a broad sampling of cases and an examination of hundreds of documents, including court records, military commission transcripts and medical assessments. The Times interviewed more than 100 people, including former detainees in a dozen countries. A full accounting is all but impossible because many former prisoners never had access to outside doctors or lawyers, and any records about their interrogation treatment and health status remain classified.

Researchers caution that it can be difficult to determine cause and effect with mental illness. Some prisoners of the C.I.A. and the military had underlying psychological problems that may have made them more susceptible to long-term difficulties; others appeared to have been remarkably resilient. Incarceration, particularly the indefinite detention without charges that the United States devised, is inherently stressful. Still, outside medical consultants and former government officials said they saw a pattern connecting the harsh practices to psychiatric issues.

Those treating prisoners at Guantánamo for mental health issues typically did not ask their patients what had happened during their questioning. Some physicians, though, saw evidence of mental harm almost immediately.

"My staff was dealing with the consequences of the interrogations without knowing what was going on," said Albert J. Shimkus, a retired Navy captain who served as the commanding officer of the Guantánamo hospital in the prison's early years. Back then, still reeling from the Sept. 11 attacks, the government was desperate to stave off more.

But Captain Shimkus now regrets not making more inquiries. "There was a conflict," he said, "between our medical duty to our patients and our duty to the mission, as soldiers."

After prisoners were released from American custody, some found neither help nor relief. Mohammed Abdullah Saleh al-Asad, a business-man in Tanzania, and others were snatched, interrogated and impris-oned, then sent home without explanation. They returned to their families deeply scarred from interrogations, isolation and the shame of sexual taunts, forced nudity, aggressive body cavity searches and being kept in diapers.

Mr. Asad, who died in May, was held for more than a year in sev-eral secret C.I.A. prisons. "Sometimes, between husband and wife, he would admit to how awful he felt," his widow, Zahra Mohamed, wrote in a statement prepared for the African Commission on Human and Peo-ples' Rights. "He was humiliated, and that feeling never went away."

'A HUMAN MOP'

In a cold room once used for interrogations at Guantánamo, Stephen N. Xenakis, a former military psychiatrist, faced a onetime Qaeda child soldier, Omar Khadr. It was December 2008, and this evaluation had been two years in the making.

The doctor, a retired brigadier general who had overseen several military hospitals, had not sought the assignment. The son of an Air Force combat veteran, he debated even accepting it. "I'm still a soldier,"

General Xenakis recalls thinking. Was this good for the country? When he finally agreed, he told Mr. Khadr's lawyers that they were paying for an independent medical opinion, not a hired gun.

Mr. Khadr, a Canadian citizen, had been wounded and captured in a firefight at age 15 at a suspected terrorist compound in Afghanistan, where he said he had been sent to translate for foreign fighters by his father, a Qaeda member. Years later, he would plead guilty to war crimes, including throwing a grenade that killed an Army medic. At the time, though, he was the youngest prisoner at Guantánamo.

He told his lawyers that the American soldiers had kept him from sleeping, spit in his face and threatened him with rape. In one meeting with the psychiatrist, Mr. Khadr, then 22, began to sweat and fan himself, despite the air-conditioned chill. He tugged his shirt off, and General Xenakis realized that he was witnessing an anxiety attack.

When it happened again, Mr. Khadr explained that he had once urinated during an interrogation and soldiers had dragged him through the mess. "This is the room where they used me as a human mop," he said.

General Xenakis had seen such anxiety before, decades earlier, as a young psychiatrist at Letterman Army Medical Center in California. It was often the first stop for American prisoners of war after they left Vietnam. The doctor recalled the men, who had endured horrific abuses, suffering panic attacks, headaches and psychotic episodes.

That session with Mr. Khadr was the beginning of General Xenakis's immersion into the treatment of detainees. He has reviewed medical and interrogation records of about 50 current and former prisoners and examined about 15 of the detainees, more than any other outside psychiatrist, colleagues say.

General Xenakis found that Mr. Khadr had post-traumatic stress disorder, a conclusion the military contested. Many of General Xenakis's diagnoses in other cases remain classified or sealed by court order, but he said he consistently found links between harsh American interrogation methods and psychiatric disorders.

Back home in Virginia, General Xenakis delved into research on the effects of abusive practices. He found decades of papers on the issue — science that had not been considered when the government began crafting new interrogation policies after Sept. 11.

At the end of the Vietnam War, military doctors noticed that former prisoners of war developed psychiatric disorders far more often than other soldiers, an observation also made of former P.O.W.s from World War II and the Korean War. The data could not be explained by imprisonment alone, researchers found. Former soldiers who suffered torture or mistreatment were more likely than others to develop long-term problems.

By the mid-1980s, the Veterans Administration had linked such treatment to memory loss, an exaggerated startle reflex, horrific nightmares, headaches and an inability to concentrate. Studies noted similar symptoms among torture survivors in South Africa, Turkey and Chile. Such research helped lay the groundwork for how American doctors now treat combat veterans.

"In hindsight, that should have come to the fore" in the post-Sept. 11 interrogation debate, said John Rizzo, the C.I.A.'s top lawyer at the time. "I don't think the long-term effects were ever explored in any real depth."

Instead, the government relied on data from a training program to resist enemy interrogators, called SERE, for Survival, Evasion, Resistance and Escape. The military concluded there was little evidence that disrupted sleep, near-starvation, nudity and extreme temperatures harmed military trainees in controlled scenarios.

Two veteran SERE psychologists, James Mitchell and Bruce Jessen, worked with the C.I.A. and the Pentagon to help develop interrogation tactics. They based their strategies in part on the theory of "learned helplessness," a phrase coined by the American psychologist Martin E. P. Seligman in the late 1960s. He gave electric shocks to dogs and discovered that they stopped resisting once they learned they could not stop the shocks. If the United States could make men helpless, the thinking went, they would give up their secrets.

In the end, Justice Department lawyers concluded that the methods did not constitute torture, which is illegal under American and international law. In a series of memos, they wrote that no evidence existed that "significant psychological harm of significant duration, e.g., lasting for months or even years" would result.

With fear of another terrorist attack, there was little incentive or time to find contrary evidence, Mr. Rizzo said. "The government wanted a solution," he recalled. "It wanted a path to get these guys to talk."

The question of what ultimately happened to Dr. Seligman's dogs never arose in the legal debate. They were strays, and once the studies were over, they were euthanized.

A SENSE OF DROWNING

Mohamed Ben Soud cannot say for certain when the Americans began using ice water to torment him. The C.I.A. prison in Afghanistan, known as the Salt Pit, was perpetually dark, so the days passed imperceptibly.

The United States called the treatment "water dousing," but the term belies the grisly details. Mr. Ben Soud, in court documents and interviews, described being forced onto a plastic tarp while naked, his hands shackled above his head. Sometimes he was hooded. One C.I.A. official poured buckets of ice water on him as others lifted the tarp's corners, sending water splashing over him and causing a choking or drowning sensation. He said he endured the treatment multiple times.

Mr. Ben Soud was among the early captives in the C.I.A.'s network of prisons in Afghanistan, Thailand, Poland, Romania and Lithuania. Again and again, he said, he told the American interrogators that he was not their enemy. A Libyan, he said he had fled to Pakistan in 1991 and joined an armed Islamist movement aimed at toppling Col. Muammar el-Qaddafi's dictatorship. Pakistani and United States officials stormed his home and arrested him in 2003. Under interrogation, he said, he denied knowing or fighting with Osama bin Laden or two senior Qaeda operatives.

In 2004, the C.I.A. turned Mr. Ben Soud over to Libya, which imprisoned him until the United States helped topple the Qaddafi government seven years later. In interviews, he and other Libyans said they were treated better by Colonel Qaddafi's jailers than by the C.I.A.

Today, Mr. Ben Soud, 47, is a free man, but said he is in constant fear of tomorrow. He is racked with self-doubt and struggles to make simple decisions. His moods swing dramatically.

" 'Dad, why did you suddenly get angry?' 'Why did you suddenly snap?' " Mr. Ben Soud said his children ask. " 'Did we do anything that made you angry?' "

Explaining would mean saying that the Americans kept him shackled in painful contortions, or that they locked him in boxes — one the size of a coffin, the other even smaller, he said in a phone interview from his home in Misurata, Libya. They slammed him against the wall and chained him from the ceiling as the prison echoed with the sounds of rock music.

"How can you explain such things to children?" he asked.

Mr. Ben Soud, along with a second former C.I.A. prisoner and the estate of a third, is suing Dr. Mitchell and Dr. Jessen in federal court, accusing them of violating his rights by torturing him. In court documents, Dr. Mitchell and Dr. Jessen argue, among other things, that they played no role in the interrogations.

Mr. Ben Soud was one of the men identified in a 2014 Senate Intelligence Committee report as having been subjected to the C.I.A.'s "enhanced interrogation techniques." Condemning the methods as brutal and ineffective in extracting intelligence, the report noted that interrogators also used unapproved tactics such as mock executions, threats to harm prisoners' children or rape their family members, and "rectal feeding," which involved inserting liquid food supplements or purées into the rectum.

Senate investigators did not set out to study the psychological consequences of the harsh treatment, but their unclassified summary revealed several cases of men suffering hallucinations, depression, paranoia and other symptoms. The full 6,000-page classified report offers many more examples, said Daniel Jones, a former F.B.I. analyst who led the Senate investigation.

"The records we reviewed clearly indicate a connection between their treatment in C.I.A. custody and their mental state," Mr. Jones said in an interview.

At least 119 men moved through the C.I.A. jails, where the interrogations were designed to disrupt the senses and increase helplessness — factors that researchers decades earlier had said could make people more susceptible to psychological harm. Forced nudity, sensory deprivation and endless light or dark were considered routine.

Many of those men were later released without charges, unsure of why they were held. About one in four prisoners should never have been captured, or turned out to have been misidentified by the C.I.A., Senate investigators concluded. Khaled el-Masri, a German citizen, is the best known case.

Macedonian authorities arrested him while he was on vacation in December 2003 and turned him over to the C.I.A. Mr. Masri said officials beat him, stripped him, forced a suppository into him and flew him to a black site in Afghanistan. He was held for months, he said, in a concrete cell with no bed, and endured more beatings and interrogations.

Years later, Mr. Masri's nightmares are accompanied by a paralyzing tightness in his chest, he said. "I have been suffering from absent-mindedness, amnesia, inability to memorize, depression, helplessness, apathy, loss of interest in the future, slow thinking, and anxiety," Mr. Masri wrote in an email.

Ms. Mohamed, the widow of Mr. Asad, the Tanzanian businessman, said he returned home paranoid and anxious.

"He used to forget things that he never would have forgotten before," she wrote recently. "For example, he would talk with someone on the phone and later forget to whom he had been talking."

Mr. Asad believed the C.I.A. seized him because he once rented space in a building he owned to Al Haramain Foundation, a Saudi charity later linked to financing terrorism. Interrogators questioned him repeatedly about the charity, he said in legal papers, then released him with no explanation.

"Mohammed's personality changed after his detention," his wife wrote. "Something tiny would happen and he would blow up — he would be so angry — I had never ever seen him like this before. At these times, he would come close to crying, and he would withdraw to be alone."

'STILL LIVING IN GITMO'

Today at Guantánamo Bay, the Caribbean landscape is reclaiming the relics of the American detention system. Weeds overtake fences in abandoned areas of the prison complex. Guard towers sit empty. It is eerily quiet.

President Obama banned coercive questioning on his second day in office and his administration has whittled the prison population to 61, down from nearly 700 at its peak. Interrogations ended long ago. Except for the so-called high-value detainees, kept in a building hidden in the hills, most of the remaining prisoners share a concrete jail called Camp 6.

Asked about their psychological well-being, Rear Adm. Peter J. Clarke, the commander at Guantánamo, said in an interview: "What I observe are detainees who are well adjusted, and I see no indications of ill effects of anything that may have happened in the past."

In the early years of Guantánamo, interrogators used variations on some of the C.I.A.'s tactics. The result was a combination of psychological and physical pressure that the International Committee of the Red Cross found was "tantamount to torture."

Capt. Richard Quattrone of the Navy, who left his post as the prison's chief medical officer in September, said his staff mostly dealt with detainees' anxiety over whether they would be released. "I've talked to some of my predecessors," he said in an interview, "and from what they say, it's vastly different today."

About 20 detainees are cleared for release. Another 10 are being prosecuted or have already been convicted in military commissions.

The fate of the remaining men, including some of the high-value prisoners, is unclear. For now they are considered too dangerous to release, but have not been charged.

For some men who have been released, Guantánamo is not easily left behind. Mr. Chekkouri, a Moroccan living in Afghanistan in 2001, was held for years as a suspected member of a group linked to Al Qaeda. He said he was beaten repeatedly at a United States military jail in Kandahar and forced to watch soldiers do the same to his younger brother.

Mr. Chekkouri is a Sufi, a member of a mystical Islamic sect that has been oppressed by Al Qaeda and others. At Guantánamo, he was kept in isolation.

When he asserted his innocence, he said, interrogators threatened to turn him over to the Moroccan authorities, who have a history of torture. The Americans warned that his family in Morocco could be jailed and abused, he said, and showed him execution photos. Interrogators repeatedly made him believe his transfer was imminent, he said. "It's time to say goodbye," interrogation files cited in court documents say. "Morocco wants you back."

After he was released last year, the United States gave him a letter saying it no longer stood by information that he was a member of a Qaeda-linked group in Morocco. Despite diplomatic assurances that he would face no charges, Morocco jailed him for several months late last year and he continues to fight allegations that he thought were behind him.

Now, he is under a psychiatrist's care and takes antidepressants and anti-anxiety drugs. He complains of flashbacks, persistent nightmares and panic attacks. He also suffers an embarrassing inability to urinate until it becomes painful. It started, he said, when he was left chained for hours during interrogations and soiled himself. His doctors say there is nothing they can treat.

"They tell me everything is normal," he said. "Your brain is playing games. It is something mental. You're still living in Gitmo. It's fear."

Mr. Chekkouri saw psychiatrists at Guantánamo, but he said he did not trust them. He and others believed the doctors shared information about medical problems with interrogators. In one case, a psychiatrist prescribed the antipsychotic medication olanzapine to a prisoner. He then suggested that interrogators exploit a side effect, food cravings, according to another military doctor who later reviewed the records.

Normally, such information would be confidential, but Guantánamo's dual missions of caring for prisoners and extracting information created conflicts. Over time, the military created two mental health teams. One, led by psychiatrists, was there to heal. The other, called the Behavioral Science Consultation Team, was led by psychologists with a very different mission.

On Sept. 3, 2003, after a teenager named Mohammed Jawad was seen talking to a poster on the wall, an interrogator called for a consultation with a BSCT (pronounced "Biscuit") psychologist. Mohammed's age at the time is in dispute. The military says it captured him at 17; his lawyer says he was more likely 14 or younger. However old, he was pleading for his mother.

When the psychologist arrived, the goal was not to ease the young man's distress, but to exploit it.

"The detainee comes across as a very immature, dependent individual, claiming to miss his mother and his young siblings, but his demeanor looks like it is a resistance technique," the psychologist wrote, according to notes seen by The Times. "He tries to look as if he is so sad that he is depressed. During today's interrogation, he appeared to be rather frightened, and it looks as if he could easily break."

The psychologist, who was not identified in the notes, recommended that Mr. Jawad be kept away from anyone who spoke his language. "Make him as uncomfortable as possible," the psychologist advised. "Work him as hard as possible."

The guards placed him in isolation for 30 days. They then subjected him to the "frequent flier program," a method of sleep deprivation.

Guards yanked Mr. Jawad from cell to cell 112 times, waking him an average of every three hours, day and night, for two weeks straight, according to court records.

After being held for years, Mr. Jawad was charged in 2007 with throwing a grenade that wounded American soldiers. But the evidence collapsed. The military prosecutor, Lt. Col. Darrel Vandeveld, withdrew from the case and declared that there was no evidence to justify charges. "There is, however, reliable evidence that he was badly mistreated by U.S. authorities, both in Afghanistan and at Guantánamo, and he has suffered, and continues to suffer, great psychological harm," he wrote in a letter to the court.

Katherine Porterfield, a New York University psychologist, found Mr. Jawad to have PTSD after examining him in 2009. Seven years after his capture, she said, he suffered from flashbacks and anxiety attacks. A panel of military doctors disagreed. Medical records from Guantánamo include repeated notes such as "no psych issues at this time," or the prisoner "denied any psych problem."

The military dropped all charges against Mr. Jawad, who is now living in Pakistan. He declined to discuss his mental health. But in a series of text messages, he wrote: "They tortured us in jails, gave us severe physical and mental pain, bombarded our villages, cities, mosques, schools." He added, "Of course we have" flashbacks, panic attacks and nightmares.

IGNORING A LINK

It has been difficult to determine the scale of mental health problems at Guantánamo, much less how many cases are linked to the treatment the prisoners endured. Most medical records remain classified. Anecdotal accounts, though, have emerged over the years.

Andy Davidson, a retired Navy captain who served as the chief psychologist treating prisoners at Guantánamo from July to October 2003, said most appeared to be in good health, but he still saw "an awful lot" of mental health issues there.

"There were definitely guys who had PTSD symptoms," he said in an interview. "There were definitely guys who had poor sleeping, nightmares. There were guys who were definitely shell shocked with a thousand-mile stare. There were guys who were depressed, avoidant."

One of the few official glimpses into the population came in a 2006 medical journal article. Two military psychologists and a psychiatrist at Guantánamo wrote that about 11 percent of detainees were then receiving mental health services, a rate lower than that in civilian jails or among former American prisoners of war. The authors acknowledged, however, that Guantánamo doctors faced significant challenges in diagnosing mental illness, most notably the difficulty in building trust. Many prisoners, including some with serious mental health conditions, refused evaluation and treatment, the study noted, which would have lowered the count.

Five years later, General Xenakis and Vincent Iacopino, the medical director for Physicians for Human Rights, published research about nine prisoners who exhibited psychological symptoms after undergoing interrogation tactics — a hose forced into a mouth, a head held in a toilet, death threats — by American jailers.

The two based their study on the medical records and interrogation files of the prisoners, all of whom had arrived at Guantánamo in its first year, had never been in C.I.A. custody, and were never charged with any crimes. In none of those cases, the study said, did Guantánamo doctors document any inquiries into whether the symptoms were tied to interrogation tactics.

Today in Tangier, Morocco, Ahmed Errachidi runs two restaurants, has a wife and five children and has been free for nearly a decade. The United States military once asserted that he trained at a Qaeda camp in early 2001, but the human rights group Reprieve later produced pay stubs showing that he had been working at the time as a cook in London.

Mr. Errachidi had a history of bipolar disorder before arriving at Guantánamo, and after being held in isolation there, he said, he suffered a psychotic breakdown. He told interrogators that he had been Bin Laden's superior officer and warned that a giant snowball would overtake the world.

Guantánamo still lurks around corners. Recently, at a market in Tangier, the clink of a chain caused a paralyzing flashback to the prison, where Mr. Errachidi was forced into painful stress positions, deprived of sleep and isolated. On chilly nights, when the blanket slips off, he is once again lying naked in a frigid cell, waiting for his next interrogation.

"All I can think of is when are they going to take me back," Mr. Errachidi said in an interview. He compared his treatment by the Americans to being mugged by a trusted friend. "It is very, very scary when you are tortured by someone who doesn't believe in torture," he said. "You lose faith in everything."

Guantánamo, particularly during its early years, operated on a system of rewards and punishments to exploit prisoners' vulnerabilities. That manipulation, taken to extremes, could have dangerous effects, as in the peculiar case of Tarek El Sawah.

An Egyptian who said he was a Taliban soldier, Mr. Sawah was captured while fleeing bombing in Afghanistan in 2001 and turned over to the United States. He arrived at Guantánamo in May 2002. Though his brother, Jamal, said he had no history of mental problems, Mr. Sawah began shrieking at night, terrified by hallucinations.

When he began defecating and urinating on himself, soldiers would hose him down in front of other detainees, a nearby prisoner stated in court documents. Mr. Sawah said he was given antipsychotic drugs, sometimes forcibly.

After his breakdown, interrogators found Mr. Sawah eager to talk. " 'Bring me good things to eat,' " he told them. They delivered McDonald's hamburgers or Subway sandwiches, multiple servings at a time.

Mr. Sawah became a prized informant, though the value of what he offered is disputed, and he says he fabricated stories, including that he was a Qaeda member. He ballooned from about 215 pounds to well over 400 pounds, records show. When the interrogations ended and he

Tarek El Sawah has headaches, mood fluctuations and eating compulsions.

was placed in a special hut for cooperators, the food kept coming. His jailers had to install a double-wide door for him.

Mr. Sawah called it a competition between the interrogators, who used food as an incentive, and the doctors, who told him to lose weight. He developed coronary artery disease, diabetes, breathing disorders and other health problems, court records show.

In 2013, General Xenakis examined him and, in a plea for better medical treatment, told a judge that "Mr. El Sawah's mental state has worsened and he appears apathetic with diminished will to live." The military responded that he was offered excellent medical care but refused it.

Today in Bosnia, Mr. Sawah, 58, complains of frequent headaches and begs a doctor for antidepressants. His mood fluctuates wildly. Though he has lost weight, his eating remains compulsive. Over dinner with a reporter after a daily Ramadan fast, he ate a steak, French fries, a plate of dates and figs, a bowl of chicken soup, spinach pie, slices of bread, the uneaten portion of another steak, another bowl of soup, two lemonades, a Coke and nearly an entire cheese plate, six or seven slices at a time.

"He's unbalanced," said his brother, who lives in New York. "He needs care. Mental care. Physical care."

Mr. Sawah does not blame American soldiers for his treatment. "They were afraid of me, afraid for their life," he said. "Guantánamo on both sides was just very scared people who want to live."

COMPLICATING TRIALS

In a war-crimes courtroom at Guantánamo Bay in January 2009, five men sat accused of plotting the Sept. 11 attacks. They were avowed enemies of the United States, who had admitted to grievous bloodshed. They had also been subjected to the most horrific of the government's interrogation tactics.

During a courtroom break, one of the men, Ammar al-Baluchi, asked to speak with a doctor. Xavier Amador, a New York psychologist who was consulting for another defendant, met with him. As they talked, Mr. Baluchi's eyes darted around the room, according to a summary of Dr. Amador's notes obtained by The Times. Mr. Baluchi said he struggled to focus, described "terrifying anxiety" and reported difficulty sleeping.

Dr. Amador noted that Mr. Baluchi seemed to meet the criteria for PTSD, anxiety disorder and major depression. "No one can live like this," Mr. Baluchi told him.

Mr. Baluchi, 39, was captured by Pakistani officers in April 2003. Though he was described as willing to talk, the C.I.A. moved him to a secret prison and immediately applied interrogation methods reserved for recalcitrant prisoners. In court documents and Mr. Baluchi's handwritten letters, he described being naked and dehydrated, chained to the ceiling so only his toes touched the floor. He endured ice-water dousing and said he was beaten until he saw flashes of light and lost consciousness. He recalls punches from his guards whenever he drifted asleep.

Today, his lawyer said, Mr. Baluchi associates sleep with imminent pain. "Not only did they not let me sleep," Mr. Baluchi wrote in a letter provided by the lawyer, "they trained me to keep myself awake."

Guantánamo physicians have prescribed Mr. Baluchi antidepressants, anti-anxiety drugs and sleeping pills, according to his lawyer, James G. Connell III, who sends him deodorants and colognes to keep flashbacks at bay. "The whole time he was in C.I.A. custody, you're sitting there, smelling your own stink," Mr. Connell said. "Now, whenever he catches a whiff of his own body odor, it sets him off."

General Xenakis, who is consulting on the case, found that Mr. Baluchi had PTSD and that he showed possible signs of a brain injury that may be linked to his beatings. He said Mr. Baluchi needed a brain scan, which the military opposes. The test would likely prompt more hearings, which could further complicate a trial.

"Having caused these problems in the first place, now the United States has to deal with them at the military commissions," Mr. Connell said. "And that takes time."

The compromised mental status of several other prisoners, like Mr. Baluchi, has affected the military proceedings against them.

Ramzi bin al-Shibh, who admits helping plan the Sept. 11 attacks, has said he believes the military is tormenting him with vibrations, smells and sounds at Guantánamo. Military doctors there have found him to be delusional, and records indicate that his symptoms began in C.I.A. custody, after brutal tactics and years of solitary confinement.

But Mr. bin al-Shibh refused to meet with doctors to assess his competency and insists he is sane, so the case continues.

Lawyers have similarly raised questions about Abd al-Nashiri's psychological state. Accused in the U.S.S. Cole bombing, he was subjected to waterboarding, mock execution, rectal feeding and other techniques — some approved, some not — at C.I.A. sites. Even after internal warnings that Mr. Nashiri was about to go "over the edge psychologically," the C.I.A. pressed forward.

Over the years, government doctors have diagnosed Mr. Nashiri with anxiety, major depression and PTSD. His lawyers do not dispute his competency to stand trial, though no such trial is imminent. His torture and mental decline, though, could make it harder for prosecutors to win a death sentence.

When the Walter Reed doctors evaluated Mr. Nashiri, "they concluded that he suffers from chronic, complex, untreated PTSD," his lawyer told a military judge in 2014. "And they attributed it to his time in C.I.A. custody."

INTERROGATION'S SHADOW

In Libya today, a former C.I.A. prisoner named Salih Hadeeyah al-Daeiki struggles to focus, and his memory fails him. He finds himself confusing the names of his children. Sometimes, he withdraws from his family to be alone.

A survivor of the C.I.A. interrogation in the Salt Pit, Mr. Daeiki says he was kept naked, humiliated and chained to the wall as loud music blared. Sleep is difficult now, but when it comes, his interrogators haunt him there.

"Something is strangling me or I'm falling from high," he said in an interview. "Or sometimes I see ghosts following me, chasing me."

Last year, a video surfaced showing Colonel Qaddafi's son, Saadi, being blindfolded and forced to listen to what sounded like the screams of other prisoners inside Al Hadba, a prison holding members of the former regime — Libya's own high-value detainees. Someone beat the soles of his feet with a stick.

As the scene unfolded, Mr. Daeiki appeared on the screen.

The beating was a mistake, he later acknowledged, but he did nothing to stop it. The goal was to collect intelligence to prevent bloodshed, he said.

He was an interrogator now.

Reporting was contributed by JAWAD SUKHANYAR from Kabul, Afghanistan; RAMI NAZZAL from Jerusalem; NOUR YOUSSEF from Cairo; HWAIDA SAAD from Beirut, Lebanon; MAHER SAMAAN from Paris; SULIMAN ALI ZWAY from Berlin; and KARAM SHOUMALI from Istanbul. KITTY BENNETT and ALAIN DELAQUÉRIÈRE contributed research.

CHAPTER 4

The Humanitarian Impact of War

When we think of humanitarian crises like famine and disease, we typically assume they occur because of a lack of development. However, today these problems are largely human-made byproducts of war, which cuts off access to food, water and sanitation. Famine and epidemics are twin effects of conflict, because malnourished populations are much more vulnerable to disease. Today, such a situation is occurring in Yemen. The Yemen war, in which the United States plays a role, risks becoming the worst humanitarian crisis in decades.

Deadly Epidemic Emerges in Sudan

BY JAMES C. MCKINLEY JR. | JULY 18, 1997

TAMBURA, THE SUDAN, JULY 16 — Dr. Michaleen Richer and her crew set up their laboratory outside a dilapidated clinic in a village of mud huts bathed in the forest's dappled light.

One by one, Dr. Richer drew blood samples from vials, mixed them with a protein and squeezed them from a dropper onto cards in a rotating machine powered by her car battery. More than eighty ragged people from the Zande village of Baragu watched and waited. Some stood sullenly in line to give blood. Others sat under trees, waiting for the news they dreaded.

"That's another positive," Dr. Richer said, pointing to one of the samples on the card. "Number ten-thirty-two."

For weeks, Dr. Richer, an American, and aid workers from CARE International have been trying to determine the extent of an outbreak of sleeping sickness that is spreading quickly through the villages here in the southwestern part of the Sudan along the border of the Central African Republic.

The preliminary results are frightening. As the civil war in the Sudan grinds into its 15th year, sleeping sickness, a parasitic malady that is fatal but curable, is once again raging through Western Equatoria province, infecting at least one in five people in Tambura County alone, doctors say. The outbreak is among the worst documented this century, doctors say, and it has even been found in villages where it has never been seen before. But because studies so far have been limited, it is impossible to know how widespread the epidemic might be.

"It's catastrophic, actually, to be truthful," said Dr. Richer, who works for the International Medical Corps, a relief organization.

This form of sleeping sickness, or African Trypanosomiasis, spread by tsetse flies, is only found in Africa within 10 degrees north and south of the equator, a region with 55 million inhabitants. The flies carry a parasite, the trypanosome, from human to human. Within three to six months, this parasite multiplies in the blood and lymph nodes, causing fever, weakness, sweating, pain in the joints and stiffness. In two to three years, the parasites migrate to the brain. There they cause personality changes, madness, and seizures. If the disease is untreated, the patient eventually slips into a coma and dies.

The surging epidemic in Tambura County is a case study in the way disease follows war in Africa, as surely as hyenas follow lions after a kill. By 1989, after more than a decade of work, Belgian doctors had pushed the incidence of sleeping sickness down to less than one percent of the population.

But when Sudanese rebels swarmed into Western Equatoria in 1990, the Belgian doctors pulled out, along with almost all of the Sudanese Government's medical staff. Then the drawn-out war severed the main trade routes to Khartoum and the rest of East Africa.

As the region became cut off from the outside world, its handful of clinics and hospitals closed down for lack of staff and medicine. No one received any medical treatment until Western charities re-established a skeletal system of clinics in 1994.

"There was a complete breakdown of health services from 1990 until the time that CARE came," said Edward Losio, a 36-year-old Sudanese lab technician who worked with the Belgian doctors. "People were not diagnosed in time. The health personnel went to exile."

To make matters worse, tens of thousands of people fled into the bush to escape the fighting, away from the towns and main roads. Thousands crossed into Congo, formerly Zaire, and the Central African Republic. The farther into the wild the people pushed, the more they were bitten by tsetse flies.

Now the disease has returned with a vengeance. Last August, nurses employed by CARE began to see hundreds of people suffering from what looked like sleeping sickness stumbling into the clinic in Ezo, about 40 miles south of the town of Tambura. More than 100 people died, but the nurses had no means to test for sleeping disease.

"So many people were dying, and we thought it was a different disease," Francis Dawa, one of the nurses in Ezo, said. "Every family is hit. Even myself, I am positive, but I'm treating the people." Because of the cost and shortage of medicine, some infected medical personnel have not yet been treated.

At the main hospital in the town of Tambura, it became clear an epidemic was rising, doctors said. In 1995, the staff there treated only 18 patients for the disease, but the number shot up to 87 in 1996. So far this year, they have admitted more than 100.

Alarmed by the numbers, Dr. Richer and Dr. Mario Enrile of CARE did a quick survey in Ezo, finding that more than a quarter of the residents were infected. In April, they persuaded the Centers for Disease Control and Prevention in Atlanta to send in a team to help do a more scientific study.

The study was interrupted for a month when rebel soldiers

harassed the researchers, but it resumed two weeks ago. The preliminary results suggest that 21 percent of the 21,500 people in villages around Ezo have the disease, Dr. Richer said. The epicenter of the outbreak appears to be in Ezo itself, where 37 percent of the 440 people who have been tested are infected.

"That means that of the 8,000 people in Ezo, about 3,000 are going to die unless we treat them," Dr. Richer said.

Epidemics have periodically swept through the region throughout its history. The local authorities say that at least 200,000 died of the illness in outbreaks between 1915 and 1940. In Uganda, an epidemic killed four million people in 1906. There are some towns in the Central African Republic — Bassigbiri for instance — that have literally been wiped out by the illness.

The disease is curable. The problem is cost. Two drugs are available that can kill the parasite, but the one prescribed for the early stages, Pentamidine, has become expensive because it is in high demand among AIDS patients. The drug itself costs only $11.50, but the cost to produce a course of treatment is between $170 and $520. The drug used in the second stage, Melarsoprol, costs about $100 for a course of treatment.

To stop the parasite's spread, all 30,000 residents in Tambura County would need to be tested, doctors here say. Then drugs would have to be administered to those who have the parasite, a project doctors estimate could cost more than $1 million.

But even those measures would not be enough. Doctors here have studied only villages in the Sudan, but it stands to reason the disease is spreading rapidly in Congo and the Central African Republic as well. Both of those countries have undergone civil wars and political upheavals recently.

"We need to treat all the people who are infected," Dr. Richer said. "There needs to be a regional control program set up." Once the study is completed, aid workers say they hope to raise international contributions to pay for the medicine to bring the epidemic under control.

In Ezo, nearly every family has been hit by the disease. Since no official record of deaths is kept, it is impossible to say precisely how many have died.

What is certain is that the recent survey has terrified Ezo's residents. Peter Lissan, a 48-year-old teacher, had brought three of his children to the clinic at Ezo. The children had been tested during the survey and were all infected. His 13-year-old daughter was very weak. She slept constantly and was unable to do the chores on the family farm, he said.

As he looked for someone to help his children, Mr. Lissan said he was sure the rest of his family had been infected as well.

"When I see the baby in the morning, and it takes time for it to wake up, I fear it is sick," he said.

"We don't call it sickness, we call it death."

The hospital in Tambura houses more advanced cases in a squalid ward of narrow beds. All are weak. Some are disoriented. On one bed, a farmer complains, "My head is evaporating."

One of the patients, a 15-year-old girl, Juhana Jima, lies half paralyzed on a sheetless mattress. She weighs only 46 pounds. Her eyes are wide, intelligent and frightened, but she is mute.

"When she came in, she couldn't eat or talk," a nurse says. "She could not get up by herself and she was always sleeping." She is being treated and will survive, but may have permanent brain damage.

Further down the ward, Carlo Bageyopai, a 44-year-old farmer from Ezo, hovers tenderly over his wife, Zaneta Siata, who is 43. The woman has also shrunk to skin and bones. She can barely talk or lift her head.

In December, Mr. Bageyopai carried his wife back to their farm in Ezo with medicine from the clinic, but she continued to decline, he said. It was only when the doctors came to test people for the survey that they found out the truth.

"We had heard that there was a disease called sleeping sickness, but it didn't occur to me that this was sleeping sickness," he said. "There are a lot of people who are suffering from this disease. Others have died without getting any medical attention."

Officials Fear Tuberculosis Epidemic in Camps

BY JOSEPH KAHN | OCT. 22, 2001

WASHINGTON, OCT. 21 — Even as aid workers struggle to provide enough food to countless Afghans displaced by war, drought and Taliban repression, health officials say they are increasingly concerned that both Afghanistan and Pakistan face another threat: a potential epidemic of tuberculosis.

Pakistan and Afghanistan already have high incidence of tuberculosis, with more than 350,000 people developing the disease each year. Now, the crowded refugee camps threaten to become a mass incubator of the disease, creating a health crisis that could last for years after the fighting stops, World Health Organization officials said last week.

"You put people in compressed spaces in a time of great stress — that kind of situation we fear can lead to a major epidemic," said Mario Raviglione, who supervises tuberculosis programs for the health organization. "We're going to be dealing with this for a long time unless we do something about it now."

The health organization, the World Bank, several United Nations agencies and more than a dozen nations seeking to fight tuberculosis outbreaks plan to meet in Washington this week to discuss a strategy to fight the disease around the world. The crisis in Afghanistan will be high on the agenda, Mr. Raviglione said.

Twenty-two nations, including the world's two most populous, China and India, are considered to have serious problems with tuberculosis, even though the disease is both preventable and highly treatable with proper medical care.

Worldwide, cases have soared in recent years, with some 8.7 million people developing the disease last year. About two million people died of tuberculosis last year, almost all of them in poor nations, where most people do not receive vaccinations and the sanitary conditions are not good.

A grouping of some 120 public and private groups devoted to fighting the disease has raised about half of the $9.3 billion that its members say would be required to wipe out the disease over the next five years. Aside from official sources, some private charities and individuals, including George Soros, the financier, have made tuberculosis a major focus of their philanthropy.

The problem had become so acute in Afghanistan that the health organization raised money to treat victims there despite the difficulty of administering aid under the Taliban, Mr. Raviglione said. The program had been expected to begin last month, but was disrupted by the Sept. 11 terrorist attacks in the United States and the allied response.

That effort is now focused on refugee camps, but health officials said the money they had raised — just over $1 million — is proving inadequate.

"To say that are resources are short in this area is a great understatement," Mr. Raviglione said.

U.N., Fearing a Polio Epidemic in Syria, Moves to Vaccinate Millions of Children

BY RICK GLADSTONE | OCT. 25, 2013

UNITED NATIONS OFFICIALS said Friday that they were mobilizing to vaccinate 2.5 million young children in Syria and more than eight million others in the region to combat what they fear could be an explosive outbreak of polio, the incurable viral disease that cripples and kills, which has reappeared in the war-ravaged country for the first time in more than a dozen years.

The officials said that the discovery a few weeks ago of a cluster of paralyzed young children in Deir al-Zour, a heavily contested city in eastern Syria, had prompted their alarm, and that tests conducted by both the government and rebel sides strongly suggested that the children had been afflicted with polio.

The possibility of a polio epidemic in Syria, where the once-vaunted public health system has collapsed after 31 months of political upheaval and war, came as the United Nations is increasingly struggling with the problem of how to deliver basic emergency aid to millions of deprived civilians there.

Valerie Amos, the top relief official at the United Nations, told the Security Council on Friday that combatants on both sides of the conflict had essentially ignored the Council's Oct. 2 directive that they must give humanitarian workers access to all areas in need.

Speaking to reporters afterward, Ms. Amos said she had expressed to the Council's members "my deep disappointment that the progress that we had hoped to see on the ground as a result of that statement has not happened, and in fact what we are seeing is a deepening of the crisis."

Dr. Bruce Aylward, the assistant director general for polio and emergencies at the World Health Organization, which is helping to lead the new polio vaccination effort in Syria, said officials at the agency were taking no chances and assuming that the 20 paralyzed children in Deir al-Zour were polio victims. "This is polio until proven otherwise," he said in a telephone interview from the group's headquarters in Geneva.

Despite the war, Dr. Aylward said he believed that both sides understood the urgent need for repeated vaccinations of all young children because polio can spread indiscriminately and is so difficult to eradicate. Nonetheless, he said, it remained unclear whether the vaccination effort, in all parts of Syria, would be impeded by the conflict's chaos and politics.

"The virus is the kind of virus that finds vulnerable populations," he said, "and the combination of vulnerability and low immunization coverage, that is a time bomb. There is a real risk of this exploding into an outbreak with hundreds of cases."

The World Health Organization, working with Unicef and other aid groups, has organized a plan to administer repeated oral doses of polio vaccine in concentric geographical circles, starting with children in Deir al-Zour and eventually reaching western Iraq, southern Turkey, Jordan, Israel, the Palestinian territories and Egypt. In Lebanon, home to more than 700,000 Syrian refugees, public health officials said Friday that they were undertaking a related effort to vaccinate all children under age 5.

Altogether, Dr. Aylward said, more than 10 million young children in the Middle East would get polio vaccinations over the next several weeks.

The World Health Organization has spent 25 years trying to eradicate polio. In recent years, the disease's presence had narrowed to just three countries — Nigeria, Pakistan and Afghanistan — from more than 125 when the campaign began in 1988. The virus is highly infectious and mainly affects children younger than 5. Within hours, it can cause irreversible paralysis or even death if breathing muscles are immobilized. The only effective treatment is prevention, the World

Health Organization says on its Web site, through multiple doses of a vaccine.

While the source of the Syrian polio strain remained unclear, public health experts said the jihadists who had entered Syria to fight the government of President Bashar al-Assad may have been carriers. Dr. Aylward said there were some indications that the strain had originated in Pakistan. He cited the recent discovery of the Pakistani strain in sewage in Egypt, Israel, the West Bank and Gaza.

The Syria aid crisis portrayed by Ms. Amos in her Security Council briefing reflected new levels of frustration over the Council's inability to act decisively on the conflict, despite its binding — and so far successful — Sept. 27 resolution on the dismantling of Syria's chemical weapons arsenal.

By contrast, the Council's Oct. 2 statement requesting that all combatants in Syria protect civilians and allow unfettered access for humanitarian aid has no enforcement power.

"This is a race against time," Ms. Amos said. "Three weeks have passed since the adoption of the Council's statement, with little change to report."

Ms. Amos told the Council that the Syrian government had withheld approval of more than 100 visas for United Nations staff members and members of other international aid groups, and had restricted workers from operating in areas with the greatest need. She also said as many as 2,000 armed opposition groups in Syria had made travel within the country increasingly dangerous. Kidnappings of humanitarian workers are increasingly common, she said, citing an instance last week when "we had a convoy that was ready to go, but we could not get enough drivers, as they fear for their lives."

Drought and War Heighten Threat of Not Just 1 Famine, but 4

BY JEFFREY GETTLEMAN | MARCH 27, 2017

BAIDOA, SOMALIA — First the trees dried up and cracked apart.

Then the goats keeled over.

Then the water in the village well began to disappear, turning cloudy, then red, then slime-green, but the villagers kept drinking it. That was all they had.

Now on a hot, flat, stony plateau outside Baidoa, thousands of people pack into destitute camps, many clutching their stomachs, some defecating in the open, others already dead from a cholera epidemic.

"Even if you can get food, there is no water," said one mother, Sangabo Moalin, who held her head with a left hand as thin as a leaf and spoke of her body "burning."

Another famine is about to tighten its grip on Somalia. And it's not the only crisis that aid agencies are scrambling to address. For the first time since anyone can remember, there is a very real possibility of four famines — in Somalia, South Sudan, Nigeria and Yemen — breaking out at once, endangering more than 20 million lives.

International aid officials say they are facing one of the biggest humanitarian disasters since World War II. And they are determined not to repeat the mistakes of the past.

One powerful lesson from the last famine in Somalia, just six years ago, was that famines were not simply about food. They are about something even more elemental: water.

Once again, a lack of clean water and proper hygiene is setting off an outbreak of killer diseases in displaced persons camps. So the race is on to dig more latrines, get swimming-pool quantities of clean water into the camps, and pass out more soap, more water-treatment tablets and more plastic buckets — decidedly low-tech supplies that could save many lives.

A dusty dirt road winds across a dry, stark landscape in Baidoa, Somalia.

"We underestimated the role of water and its contribution to mortality in the last famine," said Ann Thomas, a water, sanitation and hygiene specialist for Unicef. "It gets overshadowed by the food."

The famines are coming as a drought sweeps across Africa and several different wars seal off extremely needy areas. United Nations officials say they need a huge infusion of cash to respond. So far, they are not just millions of dollars short, but billions.

At the same time, President Trump is urging Congress to cut foreign aid and assistance to the United Nations, which aid officials fear could multiply the deaths. The United States traditionally provides more disaster relief than anyone else.

"The international humanitarian system is at its breaking point," said Dominic MacSorley, chief executive of Concern Worldwide, a large private aid group.

Aid officials say all the needed food and water exist on this planet in abundance — even within these hard-hit countries. But armed

"The environment didn't give time for these resilience efforts to bear fruit," Mr. Laurent said.

Ms. Thomas, the Unicef water and hygiene specialist, said that during Somalia's last famine, the deadliest areas were not the empty deserts where there was little food but the displaced-persons camps near urban areas where, comparatively speaking, there was plenty of food.

The reason was that the crowded camps became hotbeds of communicable diseases like cholera, a bacterial infection that can lead to very painful intestinal cramps, diarrhea and fatal dehydration. Cholera is often caused by dirty water and spread by exposure to contaminated feces through fingers, food and flies.

Malnutrition certainly played its part; famine victims, especially children, were compromised by a lack of nutrients. They arrived in the camps from wasted areas of the interior with their immune systems already shot.

But in the end it was poor hygiene and dirty water, Ms. Thomas said, that tugged many down.

If rivers and other relatively clean water sources start drying up, as they are right now in Somalia, this sets off an interlocking cycle of death. People start to get sick at their stomachs from the slimy or cloudy water they are forced to drink. They start fleeing their villages, hoping to get help in the towns.

Camps form. But the camps do not have enough water either, and it is hard to find a latrine or enough water for people to wash their hands. Shockingly fast, the camps become disease factories.

Water, of course, is less negotiable than food. A human being can survive weeks with nothing to eat. Five days without water means death.

Different strategies are being emphasized this time around to parry the famine. One is simply giving out cash.

United Nations agencies and private aid groups in Somalia are scaling up efforts to dole out money through a new electronic card system and by mobile phone.

Ali al-Hajaji and his wife, Mohamediah Mohammed, lost one son to hunger. Now they fear losing a second.

Those measures have inflicted a slow-burn toll: infrastructure destroyed, jobs lost, a weakening currency and soaring prices. But in recent weeks the economic collapse has gathered pace at alarming speed, causing top United Nations officials to revise their predictions of famine.

"There is now a clear and present danger of an imminent and great, big famine engulfing Yemen," Mark Lowcock, the under secretary for humanitarian affairs, told the Security Council on Tuesday. Eight million Yemenis already depend on emergency food aid to survive, he said, a figure that could soon rise to 14 million, or half Yemen's population.

"People think famine is just a lack of food," said Alex de Waal, author of "Mass Starvation" which analyzes recent man-made famines. "But in Yemen it's about a war on the economy."

The signs are everywhere, cutting across boundaries of class, tribe and region. Unpaid university professors issue desperate appeals for help on social media. Doctors and teachers are forced to sell their gold, land or cars to feed their families. On the streets of the capital, Sana, an elderly woman begs for alms with a loudspeaker.

"Help me," the woman, Zahra Bajali, calls out. "I have a sick husband. I have a house for rent. Help."

And in the hushed hunger wards, ailing infants hover between life and death. Of nearly two million malnourished children in Yemen, 400,000 are considered critically ill — a figure projected to rise by one quarter in the coming months.

"We are being crushed," said Dr. Mekkia Mahdi at the health clinic in Aslam, an impoverished northwestern town that has been swamped with refugees fleeing the fighting in Hudaydah, an embattled port city 90 miles to the south.

Flitting between the beds at her spartan clinic, she cajoled mothers, dispensed orders to medics and spoon-fed milk to sickly infants. For some it was too late: the night before, an 11-month old boy had died. He weighed five and a half pounds.

Looking around her, Dr. Mahdi could not fathom the Western obsession with the Saudi killing of Jamal Khashoggi in Istanbul.

"We're surprised the Khashoggi case is getting so much attention while millions of Yemeni children are suffering," she said. "Nobody gives a damn about them."

She tugged on the flaccid skin of a drowsy 7-year-old girl with stick-like arms. "Look," she said. "No meat. Only bones."

The embassy of Saudi Arabia in Washington did not respond to questions about the country's policies in Yemen. But Saudi officials have defended their actions, citing rockets fired across their border by the Houthis, an armed group professing Zaidi Islam, an offshoot of Shiism, that Saudi Arabia, a Sunni monarchy, views as a proxy for its regional rival, Iran.

The Saudis point out that they, along with the United Arab Emirates, are among the most generous donors to Yemen's humanitarian relief effort. Last spring, the two allies pledged $1 billion in aid to

Yemen. In January, Saudi Arabia deposited $2 billion in Yemen's central bank to prop up its currency.

But those efforts have been overshadowed by the coalition's attacks on Yemen's economy, including the denial of salaries to civil servants, a partial blockade that has driven up food prices, and the printing of vast amounts of bank notes, which caused the currency to plunge.

And the offensive to capture Hudaydah, which started in June, has endangered the main lifeline for imports to northern Yemen, displaced 570,000 people and edged many more closer to starvation.

A famine here, Mr. Lowcock warned, would be "much bigger than anything any professional in this field has seen during their working lives."

WHEN ALI HAJAJI'S SON FELL ILL with diarrhea and vomiting, the desperate father turned to extreme measures. Following the advice of village elders, he pushed the red-hot tip of a burning stick into Shaher's chest, a folk remedy to drain the "black blood" from his son.

"People said burn him in the body and it will be O.K.," Mr. Hajaji said. "When you have no money, and your son is sick, you'll believe anything."

The burns were a mark of the rudimentary nature of life in Juberia, a cluster of mud-walled houses perched on a rocky ridge. To reach it, you cross a landscape of sandy pastures, camels and beehives, strewn with giant, rust-colored boulders, where women in black cloaks and yellow straw boaters toil in the fields.

In the past, the men of the village worked as migrant laborers in Saudi Arabia, whose border is 80 miles away. They were often treated with disdain by their wealthy Saudi employers but they earned a wage. Mr. Hajaji worked on a suburban construction site in Mecca, the holy city visited by millions of Muslim pilgrims every year.

When the war broke out in 2015, the border closed.

The fighting never reached Juberia, but it still took a toll there.

Last year a young woman died of cholera, part of an epidemic that infected 1.1 million Yemenis. In April, a coalition airstrike hit a wedding party in the district, killing 33 people, including the bride. A local boy who went to fight for the Houthis was killed in an airstrike.

But for Mr. Hajaji, who had five sons under age 7, the deadliest blow was economic.

He watched in dismay as the riyal lost half its value in the past year, causing prices to soar. Suddenly, groceries cost twice as much as they had before the war. Other villagers sold their assets, such as camels or land, to get money for food.

But Mr. Hajaji, whose family lived in a one-room, mud-walled hut, had nothing to sell.

At first he relied on the generosity of neighbors. Then he pared back the family diet, until it consisted only of bread, tea and halas, a vine leaf that had always been a source of food but now occupied a central place in every meal.

Soon his first son to fall ill, Shaadi, was vomiting and had diarrhea, classic symptoms of malnutrition. Mr. Hajaji wanted to take the ailing 4-year-old to the hospital, but that was out of the question: fuel prices had risen by 50 percent over the previous year.

One morning in late September, Mr. Hajaji walked into his house to find Shaadi silent and immobile, with a yellow tinge to his skin. "I knew he was gone," he said. He kissed his son on the forehead, bundled him up in his arms, and walked along a winding hill path to the village mosque.

That evening, after prayers, the village gathered to bury Shaadi. His grave, marked by a single broken rock, stood under a grove of Sidr trees that, in better times, were famous for their honey.

Shaadi was the first in the village to die from hunger.

A few weeks later, when Shaher took ill, Mr. Hajaji was determined to do something. When burning didn't work, he carried his son down the stony path to a health clinic, which was ill-equipped for the task. Half of Yemen's health facilities are closed because of the war.

So his family borrowed $16 for the journey to the hospital in Hajjah.

"All the big countries say they are fighting each other in Yemen," Mr. Hajaji said. "But it feels to us like they are fighting the poor people."

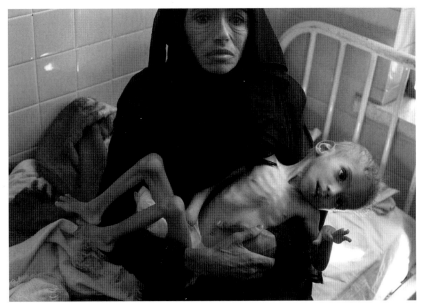

Bassam Mohammed Hassan, who suffers from severe malnutrition and cerebral palsy, at a hospital in Sana, Yemen.

YEMEN'S ECONOMIC CRISIS WAS not some unfortunate but unavoidable side effect of the fighting.

In 2016, the Saudi-backed Yemeni government transferred the operations of the central bank from the Houthi-controlled capital, Sana, to the southern city of Aden. The bank, whose policies are dictated by Saudi Arabia, a senior Western official said, started printing vast amounts of new money — at least 600 billion riyals, according to one bank official. The new money caused an inflationary spiral that eroded the value of any savings people had.

The bank also stopped paying salaries to civil servants in Houthi-controlled areas, where 80 percent of Yemenis live. With the government as the largest employer, hundreds of thousands of families in the north suddenly had no income.

At the Sabeen hospital in Sana, Dr. Huda Rajumi treats the country's most severely malnourished children. But her own family is suffering, too, as she falls out of Yemen's vanishing middle class.

In the past year, she has received only a single month's salary. Her husband, a retired soldier, is no longer getting his pension, and Dr. Rajumi has started to skimp on everyday pleasures, like fruit, meat and taxi rides, to make ends meet.

"We get by because people help each other out," she said. "But it's getting hard."

Economic warfare takes other forms, too. In a recent paper, Martha Mundy, a lecturer at the London School of Economics, analyzed coalition airstrikes in Yemen, finding that their attacks on bridges, factories, fishing boats and even fields suggested that they aimed to destroy food production and distribution in Houthi-controlled areas.

Saudi Arabia's tight control over all air and sea movements into northern Yemen has effectively made the area a prison for those who live there. In September, the World Health Organization brokered the establishment of a humanitarian air bridge to allow the sickest Yemenis — cancer patients and others with life-threatening conditions — to fly to Egypt.

Among those on the waiting list is Maimoona Naji, a 16-year-old girl with a melon-size tumor on her left leg. At a hostel in Sana, her father, Ali Naji, said they had obtained visas and money to travel to India for emergency treatment. Their hopes soared in September when his daughter was told she would be on the first plane out of Sana once the airlift started.

But the agreement has stalled, blocked by the Yemeni government, according to the senior Western official. Maimoona and dozens of other patients have been left stranded, the clock ticking on their illnesses.

"First they told us 'next week, next week,' " said Mr. Naji, shuffling through reams of documents as tears welled up in his eyes. "Then they said no. Where is the humanity in that? What did we do to deserve this?"

Airstrikes have destroyed bridges, like this one in Bani Hassan, factories, fishing boats and fields, suggesting that disrupting the food supply may have been a goal.

THE SAUDI COALITION IS NOT solely to blame for Yemen's food crisis.

In Houthi-held areas, aid workers say, commanders level illegal taxes at checkpoints and frequently try to divert international relief aid to the families of soldiers, or to line their own pockets.

At the United Nations on Tuesday, Mr. Lowcock, the humanitarian official, said that aid workers in Yemen faced obstacles including delayed visas, retracted work permits and interference in the work — problems, officials said privately, that were greatest in Houthi-held areas.

Despite the harrowing scenes of suffering in the north, some Yemenis are getting rich. Upmarket parts of Sana are enjoying a mini real estate boom, partly fueled by Yemeni migrants returned from Saudi Arabia, but also by newly enriched Houthi officials.

Local residents say they have seen Houthi officials from modest backgrounds driving around the city in Lexus four-wheel drives, or

The fighting has displaced about a million Yemenis.

shopping in luxury stores, trailed by armed gunmen, to buy suits and perfumes.

Tensions reached a climax this summer when the head of the United Nations migration agency was forced to leave Sana after clashing with the Houthi administration.

In an interview, the Houthi vice foreign minister, Hussain al-Ezzi, denied reports of corruption, and insisted that tensions with the United Nations had been resolved.

"We don't deny there have been some mistakes on our side," he said. "We are working to improve them."

ONLY TWO FAMINES HAVE BEEN OFFICIALLY DECLARED by the United Nations in the past 20 years, in Somalia and South Sudan. A United Nations-led assessment due in mid-November will determine how close Yemen is to becoming the third.

To stave it off, aid workers are not appealing for shipments of relief aid but for urgent measures to rescue the battered economy.

"This is an income famine," said Lise Grande, the United Nations humanitarian coordinator for Yemen. "The key to stopping it is to ensure that people have enough money to buy what they need to survive."

The priority should be to stabilize the falling currency, she said, and to ensure that traders and shipping companies can import the food that Yemenis need.

Above all, she added, "the fighting has to stop."

One hope for Yemenis is that the international fallout from the death of the Saudi dissident, Jamal Khashoggi, which has damaged Prince Mohammed's international standing, might force him to relent in his unyielding prosecution of the war.

Peter Salisbury, a Yemen specialist at Chatham House, said that was unlikely.

"I think the Saudis have learned what they can get away with in Yemen — that western tolerance for pretty bad behavior is quite high," he said. "If the Khashoggi murder tells us anything, it's just how reluctant people are to rein the Saudis in."

SAEED AL-BATATI contributed reporting.

Cholera, Lurking Symptom of Yemen's War, Appears to Make Roaring Comeback

BY RICK GLADSTONE | MARCH 27, 2019

CHOLERA, A POTENTIALLY FATAL DISEASE that has come to symbolize the humanitarian crisis of the war in Yemen, has surged again in the country, health workers reported Wednesday, with some areas hit by as many as 2,000 suspected or confirmed cases per week.

Doctors Without Borders, the medical charity, said in a statement that its teams had recently seen a "dramatic increase in cholera cases, demonstrating the urgent need for humanitarian assistance to improve water and sanitation in the war-torn country."

The World Health Organization said that from the beginning of 2019 through March 17, nearly 109,000 cases of severe acute watery diarrhea and suspected cholera had been reported, with nearly 200 deaths. About one-third of the reported cases afflicted children under-age 5, the organization said.

Spread by poor hygiene and contaminated drinking water, cholera can cause fatal dehydration without treatment. It has long been considered endemic to Yemen, the Arab world's poorest country.

But cholera cases exploded after the war began in March 2015 between Yemen's Houthi rebels and a Saudi-led coalition, which led to a basic collapse in public health and sanitation systems.

Two years ago Yemen suffered the world's largest cholera outbreak, with more than 1 million cases. Although the disease was brought under control, medical organizations operating in the country have continued to see cases in almost every region.

Doctors Without Borders said that its facilities had admitted more than 7,900 patients with suspected cholera in Amran, Hajjah, Ibb and Taiz governorates in western Yemen since Jan. 1.

Over the past three months, the charity said, "the number of suspected or confirmed cholera patients increased from 140 to 2,000 per week."

Hassan Boucenine, the head of the charity's Yemen mission, said the increase was particularly concerning because the rainy season, which could aggravate the problem, had not even started yet.

Dr. Ahmed Al Mandhari, the regional director of the World Health Organization, and Geert Cappelaere, the regional director for Unicef, said in a joint statement that they had begun scaling up the response "to assist immediately the people affected and to prevent the disease from spreading further."

But they also acknowledged that "we face several challenges, including the intensification of fighting, access restrictions and bureaucratic hurdles to bring lifesaving supplies and personnel to Yemen."

The United Nations considers Yemen, where the war has just entered its fifth year, to be the world's worst man-made humanitarian crisis. Relief officials have said 24 million people, close to 80 percent of Yemen's population, need protection and assistance, hunger is rampant, and famine threatens hundreds of thousands.

CHAPTER 5

Lives Unsettled by Occupation and Displacement

As places become war zones, life is thrown into disarray. People flee their homes and become internally displaced or they must leave the country altogether, as have millions of refugees from Syria. Resettling such populations often takes years, sometimes even longer. In addition, lives can be disturbed by military occupation, which often entails restricted rights and increased factional tensions. Israel and Kashmir are especially useful examples of how the problems of military occupation continue for decades.

Ethiopian Army Begins Leaving Mogadishu

BY MOHAMED IBRAHIM AND JEFFREY GETTLEMAN | JAN. 2, 2009

MOGADISHU, SOMALIA — Ethiopian Army trucks, packed with soldiers, tents, mattresses and other gear, began Friday to pull out of Mogadishu, Somalia's battle-zone of a capital, in the first signs of the expected Ethiopian withdrawal.

Many Somalis in their path immediately fled, predicting that the departing Ethiopian troops would be attacked by mines and insurgents. Almost as soon as they began to move, the Ethiopians hit a roadside bomb. At least nine civilians and an unknown number of Ethiopian soldiers were killed.

Thousands of Ethiopian troops stormed into Mogadishu two years ago in an attempt to shore up Somalia's weak transitional government and to wipe out an Islamist administration that the Ethiopians considered a terrorist threat.

But the Ethiopian occupation mostly failed. The Somali government is as divided and weak as ever. Islamist insurgents, many of them radical and violent, have seized control of much of Somalia. Thousands of civilians have been killed in relentless combat between Islamist militants and the Ethiopians, with European Union officials accusing the Ethiopians of war crimes. And millions of Somalis are on the brink of famine, the victims of war, displacement, drought and disease.

The Ethiopians were never popular in Somalia. But as people in Mogadishu watched the first convoy of 18 heavily loaded trucks chug down the bullet-pocked streets and head toward the Ethiopian border on Friday, many said they feared what would happen next.

"If the Ethiopians leave, there is a possibility of war among the Islamist fighters," said Jamal Ali, a student at Mogadishu University.

It is not clear whether the Ethiopian troops are leaving Somalia entirely or simply redeploying from Mogadishu to other areas of the country. Western diplomats estimate that several thousand Ethiopian troops remain inside Somalia, and many Somalia analysts have predicted that the Ethiopians will linger for some time inside the country or along the border as a buffer against Islamist militants.

"We have already started to implement our withdrawal plan," said Bereket Simon, a spokesman for Ethiopia's prime minister, Agence France-Presse reported. "It is a process and it will take some time."

Around 3,000 African Union peacekeepers are still in Somalia, trying to protect the few fortified enclaves that Somalia's transitional government controls. On Thursday, a little-known Islamist group, the Ras Kamboni Rebels, attacked peacekeepers in two locations, though it was not clear if any people were killed.

MOHAMMED IBRAHIM reported from Mogadishu, Somalia, and JEFFREY GETTLEMAN from Nairobi, Kenya.

In Torn Gaza, if Roof Stands, It's Now Home

BY JODI RUDOREN | AUG. 17, 2014

GAZA CITY — Telltale signs of the displaced are everywhere in Gaza. Tiny sandals are scattered on the doormat of a lawyer's office above downtown Gaza City's main street: The tiny feet belong to the children who have been living inside since July 20. Upstairs, in the dental laboratory where Mohamed Efranji fashions crowns and veneers, there are trays of onions, potatoes, red peppers and tomatoes to feed three families who now call it home.

At the Rimal Salon at the edge of the Beach refugee camp, two hairdressers have brought their 10 younger siblings to stay. On Tuesday, their mother was making macaroni on a camp stove in a mirrored back room where brides usually primp. Around the corner, a colorful blanket blocked a doorway to a long-closed Internet cafe where 13 more people have set up house in two high-ceiling rooms that lack both running water and working electric outlets.

Scores of families have hung sheets and scarves from every available tree and pole to create shady spaces on the grounds of Al Shifa Hospital; in the unauthorized camp, a 3-month-old slept one recent morning in a wire crib lined with cardboard.

On Sunday, more than 235,000 people were still crammed into 81 of the United Nations' 156 schools, where classes are supposed to start next Sunday. "The chances of that," acknowledged Scott Anderson, deputy director of the agency that runs them, "are zero."

After a month of fierce fighting between Israel and Palestinian militants that killed more than 1,900 Gaza residents, the extension of a temporary cease-fire through Monday was a great relief. But with an estimated 11,000 homes destroyed and many more severely damaged, Gaza's housing and humanitarian crises are just beginning, and the

Displaced families hung sheets and scarves to create a camp on the grounds of Al Shifa Hospital in Gaza City.

uncertainty over the timing and terms for a more durable truce makes recovery planning elusive.

"Our fate at the end will be in the street," lamented Alia Kamal Elaf, a 35-year-old mother of eight who has been staying at a school since fleeing the Shejaiya neighborhood in east Gaza City at the onset of Israel's ground incursion on July 17.

The destruction has been far more severe than in previous rounds of Israeli attacks, especially in Shejaiya, the northern border town of Beit Hanoun and the southeastern village of Khuza'a, where little at all is left. Palestinian leaders plan to ask international donors for $6 billion at a conference scheduled for September, but there are many challenges money cannot solve.

The Hamas-run government that ruled Gaza since 2007 resigned in June, but the Palestinian Authority has yet to take control of its ministries. So who will assess damage or coordinate reconstruction?

Israel currently bans the import of construction materials for private projects, citing security concerns. In any case, several of Gaza's cement-mixing plants and other factories that make doors, windows and floor tiles have been reduced to rubble.

Many aid workers think cash grants would provide the most efficient relief: People could fix homes that are still standing, rent new spaces or offset expenses as they cram in with relatives. But the United States will not give cash directly to people because it is too complicated to determine their possible connections with Hamas, which is deemed a terrorist organization by Washington.

"We'll get lots of money to rebuild homes we can't rebuild, but we won't get the money to help these people help themselves," said Robert Turner, director of Gaza operations for the United Nations Relief and Works Agency, which provides education, health and other services to the 70 percent of Gaza residents who are classified as refugees. "You cannot do widespread shelter construction unless construction material is free and available in the local market. Which it's not, and is it ever going to be?"

Turkey, Qatar and other nations have offered to send mobile homes. But Mr. Turner sees this as a wasteful step in the wrong direction. Each unit costs about $15,000, he said; the agency's standard rental subsidy in Gaza is $150 per month, or $3,600 for two years. A permanent home can be built for $40,000.

"There are three problems," Mr. Turner said. "People hate them, they're really expensive, and you set up these ghettos."

The agency is facing a similar dilemma over its shelters, where some families have now been for 36 days. About 350 children have been born at the shelters; on Wednesday, United Nations employees staged a boisterous wedding for one displaced couple. Still, there are no showers.

Mr. Anderson, Mr. Turner's deputy at Unrwa, said Thursday that he planned to start having showers installed in the coming days — at least at the 15 schools across the strip where the agency expected to keep shelters open even after the conflict officially came to a close. Already, he is placing a nurse and health educator at each site in the hope of staving off outbreaks of meningitis, lice and scabies. Soon, the agency will replace daily distribution of canned food, which costs $1.60 per person, with cheaper, twice-weekly boxes of pantry supplies.

"We cannot throw people out of the shelters," Mr. Anderson said. "It's the gray area of wanting to do the best we can to provide dignified living conditions, but also not wanting to turn the shelters into hotels where people want to stay."

There seems to be little danger of that.

People at the schools complain of incessant flies and fetid bathrooms. Ms. Elaf, the woman worried about ending up on the street, said she has but one mattress for her eight children, ages 8 to 16. Another woman staying at the same school yanked down her 7-year-old son's shorts to show an angry red sore on his thigh. The classrooms smell. Hallways are filthy and often wet. Family fights are becoming more frequent.

Conditions are worse on the grounds of Shifa Hospital, where neither food nor water is provided to the makeshift camp that sprawls outside the internal medicine building, next to the X-ray department, between the emergency room, the morgue and the maternity ward. Many of the tents are made from sheets that say "Palestinian Health Ministry" in Arabic.

The brothers Hamouda have an actual tent, provided, they said, by a "do-gooder" in week four of their stay. Half the ground is covered with cardboard, the other half with woven mats. In the corner is an old soda bottle half filled with fiery red pepper sauce, a Shejaiya standard.

"We count the days as we sit in a tent," said the youngest of the three men, Moamar, 42, on day 35.

"Here," said the middle brother, Abdullah, 45, "each day equals a year."

The oldest, Muhammad, 48, said that if the cease-fire held, he would go to the spot where the family's home was "and wait for a tent — I'll put a tent in the street and sit there."

Rubble in Beit Hanoun. Throughout Gaza, more than 235,000 people were being sheltered in 81 United Nations' schools.

But Moamar disagreed. "We will stay here until they bring a solution for us," he said. "My opinion is that we stay here, as a pressure tool."

Their wives have been staying with relatives, as an estimated 200,000 of the temporarily displaced have done. Even this, considered the best alternative, has its downside: Religious women and girls must wear long sleeves and cover their hair at all times because they are not in their own homes; many are not allowed to sit in courtyards or on stoops because they do not know the neighbors.

Those who have managed to find spots to rent said they were paying double the prewar rates: One group of 12 was pulling furniture from the Beit Hanoun rubble the other day to take to a fourth-floor unit in the Sheikh Zayed complex, with no elevator, for $200 a month. Hani Zeyara, who is from Shejaiya and slept for weeks at the makeshift Shifa Hospital camp or in a park, said he had finally found an empty store: 260 square feet for $100 a month.

Adel al-Ghoula, 28, has already pitched a tent, of sorts, in front of the pile of debris that used to be the home where he lived from the age of 13, just across the road that runs close to Gaza's eastern boundary. He used wire to tie two-by-fours to the iron fence lining the road, and then to tie colorful cloths, many of them torn or singed, to the wood. Inside, wooden pallets are propped on rocks and strewn with worn cushions, forming seats in the shade.

The date, grape, olive, fig, walnut and lemon trees are all gone. A stone arch doorway and wrought-iron gate are basically the only things left standing of what Mr. Ghoula said had been a four-story building housing six families — 50 people — as well as several first-floor businesses. Mr. Ghoula had owned two sewing machines and made women's shoes.

"This is the remains of my computer," he said, picking up a piece of black plastic. "This is my daughter's handbag." It was red, with sparkles; she is 4.

He put a sign on the pile, "Home of the al-Ghoula Family," to ward off looters, perhaps attract assessors or just signal to neighbors: We are still here.

"We must rent a place, but we should still come here every day and sit here," Mr. Ghoula said as a stranger on a donkey cart stopped for a drink of fresh water. "To receive people. To tell the world: We are rooted in our land, until death."

FARES AKRAM contributed reporting.

Inside a Jordanian Refugee Camp: Reporter's Notebook

TIMES INSIDER | BY JODI RUDOREN | SEPT. 22, 2015

Times Insider delivers behind-the-scenes insights into how news, features and opinion come together at The New York Times.

ZAATARI REFUGEE CAMP, JORDAN — When I first visited Zaatari a few months after it opened in 2012, I wrote about the emerging marketplace: a couple dozen kiosks where people hawk used clothes, snacks, SIM cards and perfume. It was one of several signs of Syrians settling in, I said then; of realizing that they would "likely live in this camp for months, not days or weeks."

On my fourth visit, last week, the story was thematically similar, only on steroids. That nascent market now has 2,500 shops. Dusty tents have been replaced by tin trailers that the refugees have assembled into family compounds and have kept spotless. Some have planted gardens and taken pets, and aid groups are installing water, sewage and solar-power systems. Returning to Syria seems a distant dream. A few are looking toward Europe, but many understand now that they are likely to live in the camp for years, not months.

It is horribly sad, but also somewhat inspirational.

If I had been bombed out of my home, I fear I would just curl up and cry. The Syrians are incredible entrepreneurs: Several said they can now find "anything we want" in the market. My Jordanian colleague, Rana F. Sweis, a Spanish photographer, Samuel Aranda, our driver and translator, Ihab Muhtaseb, and I had some delicious ice cream (about 75 cents for two scoops) made in the camp by Daoud Hariri, 30, who said his family once supplied all the shops in the Syrian town of Dara'a.

But Mr. Hariri said this summer he could keep just five flavors — chocolate, strawberry, mango, lemon and what he called "milk and cookies" — because the camp supplies electricity only for set hours each night. Using a generator, he can only afford to power a single freezer.

When I reported in Zaatari after harsh winter storms in 2013 and again later that spring, it was a chaotic, dangerous place. Filthy children walked barefoot in puddles. Riots broke out over too-few trailers; people looted stores, stole electricity, and protested against the camp management. Now it is orderly and quiet; women wear matching eye shadow, lipstick and nail polish; men and boys cruise through the camp on bicycles doing errands or odd jobs.

The camp, whose population peaked in 2013 at 156,000, according to the United Nations, now has 79,000 residents; it has been closed to newcomers since May 2014. So instead of interviewing the hordes huddling over high-protein wafers at the registration tent, we started at the crowded "returns center" where refugees apply for permits to return to Syria, try their luck on the perilous journey to Europe, or, as one woman put it, exit the camp for a "vacation" in Jordanian towns.

The Jordanian authorities have made reporting in the camp much more difficult: It takes at least 10 days to get a permit. Journalists are allowed in only from 9 a.m. to 3 p.m. and must be accompanied everywhere by a police officer — except on Fridays, the Muslim holy day, when they let us roam on our own, but asked Ihab to report what we had done.

Families welcomed us into their compounds and served us strong coffee in chipped china cups. Most seemed to have had a baby while in camp — 80 are born here each week. Issa Suleiman named his 8-month-old daughter Sham, after Damascus.

I did not hear a single one of these infants cry, and their older siblings sat quietly while I talked to their parents. At first I marveled at how much better behaved they seemed than my own twins, now 8, who so often seem unable to entertain themselves without a screen. Then I began to understand that Zaatari's children are docile because they have so little to do; they are drained — of energy, of possibility, of hope.

Walid Lebad with his family outside their trailer at the Zaatari refugee camp in Jordan. Mr. Lebad started a garden seven months ago using soil from a construction project on the camp's outskirts and water recycled from his family's bathing and cooking.

On Friday afternoon, Rana and I were waiting for Samuel and Ihab to finish photographing noon prayers at the mosque when a 15-year-old named Jihad came up and asked, "Are you interested in gardens?" He proudly showed off the parsley, mint and eggplant he had planted in pots in his family's courtyard. Inside, his father had strung a rope over a metal bar holding up the flimsy ceiling, then slung a pillow over the rope: a swing for his 7-year-old sister, Aya.

I suppose I should not be surprised that even in these dire circumstances, everyone has developed a daily routine. But Ali Al Humsi, a barber who plays the oud, guitar and recorder, described his in a poetic simplicity that stuck with me.

"At 6, 6:30, I wake up because of my daughter," Mr. Humsi, 25, said of 9-month-old Nuha, whose birth prompted him and his wife to enter Zaatari after trying for two years to scratch out a living in the Jordanian cities of Jerash and Rantha. "I make coffee, and I prepare the milk for the girl, then we sit in the courtyard. I give her the milk. Then I smoke; then I play with the baby. Then I make a sandwich, unless my wife is awake; she makes me breakfast.

"At 8, 8:30, I'm waiting for my friend. We ride the bike, and we go to the center," Mr. Humsi continued, referring to the place where the Norwegian Refugee Council pays him to teach teenagers to cut hair. "We arrive there a bit before 9. I smoke. And then I go to class. I leave at 1. I arrive here at 2. I eat lunch."

Mr. Humsi was sitting in a trailer decorated with deep purple curtains and a matching carpet. The other trailer is where they sleep. In between there is a makeshift kitchen.

"I can't sit down from the heat, so I'm moving from one caravan to the other," he said. "Then I put water on myself to cool down." He dunks the baby in a bucket.

"By now it's 4:30. I go to the barber shop. I stay until 8:30 or 9. I come home, I eat dinner. I go to evening events or parties or gatherings." Often, he hosts neighbors on the street in front of his trailer, sometimes bringing in other musicians from around the camp. He played us a mournful ballad about the importance of a mother's love while in exile.

"I come back, I sit with my wife, we drink Nescafe," Mr. Humsi continued. "We discuss whether to stay or leave. We are in conflict; sometimes it turns into a battle. It feels like a war, sometimes, these discussions. I want to leave, and she wants to stay. She just feels like it's close to Syria; she's nostalgic. I want a future for the baby. I tell her my place is not here.

"I'm comfortable. I have friends, I have neighbors. But there is an important point: I don't want to become attached.

"It's O.K. for a time, a limited time," he concluded of Zaatari. "If you don't think about the future, if you just think about today, it's fine."

Migrant Crisis Raises Issues of Refugees' Rights and Nations' Obligations

BY SOMINI SENGUPTA | SEPT. 23, 2015

THE FLOOD OF MIGRANTS and refugees into Europe this year — more than a half-million so far, many fleeing the civil war in Syria and other conflict zones — has sorely strained the Continent's ability to absorb them. Leaders argued bitterly for weeks before the European Union could adopt a plan on Tuesday to share the burden among its members.

The plan will require some countries to accept refugees and some people to be relocated whether they like it or not, raising issues of freedom, rights and obligations under international law. Here are answers to some of the key questions.

Q. *Can refugees choose where they get asylum?*

A. To a certain extent, yes. People fleeing war or persecution are free to choose where to seek asylum. Most often it will be a neighboring country or the first safe place they are able to reach, but it could also be a country halfway around the world. Under international law, nations have a legal duty not to turn refugees away; they must be allowed to apply for asylum, even if they have entered a host country's territory illegally.

But it is up to each host country to decide under its own laws whether to allow refugees to stay there permanently and whether they and their children can become citizens, among other issues.

Q. *Can host countries send refugees elsewhere?*

A. Yes, within limits. Nothing in international law prohibits countries from agreeing to distribute refugees among them, as the European

Union plans to do, in order to share the burden of accommodating arrivals while their asylum applications are considered.

There is an important caveat, though: Countries are prohibited from sending refugees to a place where they would not be protected from persecution.

For that reason, it may be hard for the European Union to justify sending refugees to a country like Hungary that has been actively hostile to accepting them, according to Madeline Garlick, a lawyer for the Migration Policy Institute in Brussels. But she said there was no bar to sending refugees who are awaiting asylum to stay in Poland, for example, even if they said they wanted to go to Germany.

Q. *Are there precedents for distributing refugees this way?*

A. When refugees began to reach Australia from Southeast Asia in large numbers, Australia tried to send some of them to Malaysia to be housed. The Australian courts struck down the arrangement because Malaysia did not have a good record of providing protection to refugees, according to James C. Hathaway, a law professor at the University of Michigan. But he said the European Union's plan was "absolutely, utterly correct and legal."

The situation in Europe is complicated by the bloc's system of open internal borders and free movement. A longstanding rule that asylum seekers should be accommodated by the first member country they entered, and can be sent back there if they go elsewhere in the union, has partly broken down under the pressure of the current wave of migrants.

Q. *Can asylum be denied? What happens then?*

A. If refugees cannot demonstrate "a well-founded fear of persecution" in the country they fled, they can be denied asylum and deported. But the refugees are entitled to a full and fair hearing first, and not a swift rejection in what the United Nations last week called "summary proceedings."

They can also be denied asylum and lose protected status as refugees if they are found to have committed war crimes or crimes against humanity.

Q. *How can refugees receive asylum in the United States?*

A. One way is to physically reach American soil. A person who then claims to be fleeing war or persecution must be allowed to make that case before a court.

Another way, for those who cannot get to America on their own, is to be referred through the United Nations refugee agency. Thousands of such applicants are granted asylum each year after being screened first by the United Nations and then by American officials, a process that generally takes 18 to 24 months. The refugees might not have chosen the United States specifically; the United Nations agency decides where to refer them. Once they are in the United States, these refugees usually get help with housing and job placement, and they can eventually become citizens.

Russia Is Trying to Wipe Out Crimea's Tatars

OPINION | BY CHRISTINA M. PASCHYN | MAY 19, 2016

RUSSIA SUFFERED AN unexpected defeat in the Eurovision Song Contest on Saturday when its singer came in third, while Ukraine, of all countries, took first place.

To add insult to injury, Ukraine's contestant, Jamala, is of Crimean Tatar descent. And she didn't sing just any song, but a song about her people's ruthless deportation by Soviet authorities in 1944, when more than 230,000 Crimean Tatars, an overwhelming majority of the population, were exiled from the Crimean Peninsula. Nearly half died as a result of this ethnic cleansing.

Russian officials criticized Ukraine's victory as yet another example of the West's "propaganda and information war" against their country. Meanwhile, Europe is no doubt feeling good about itself for delivering a karmic blow to President Vladimir V. Putin of Russia, whose annexation of Crimea in 2014 and continuing war in Ukraine still sting.

But the Eurovision victory took place in the world of entertainment. In the real world, Russia is escalating its crackdown on the Crimean Tatars, who now make up 12 percent of Crimea's population after the Soviet Union allowed the deportation survivors and their descendants to return in 1989.

On April 26, Russia banned the Crimean Tatars' legislature, the Mejlis, calling it an extremist organization. On May 12, the authorities arrested several Tatars, including Ilmi Umerov, deputy chairman of the Mejlis. Activists say that more searches and arrests are likely soon. This would be a particularly tone-deaf move on Russia's part, considering that the anniversary of the 1944 deportation is this week.

But if past treatment of the Crimean Tatars is anything to go by, Russia probably isn't bothered by that.

The Crimean Tatars have always been easy scapegoats for Russia. Joseph Stalin's justification for deporting them was that they had sided with Germany in World War II. It's true that some did, historians say, either because they were forced to by the invading army or because they believed the Germans would liberate them from the Soviet Union. But records show that just as many Crimean Tatars, if not more, did not defect during the war. Many fought valiantly for the Red Army.

Brian Glyn Williams, a historian at the University of Massachusetts at Dartmouth, posits that Stalin's true motivation wasn't revenge but instead plans to launch a war against Turkey to retake land that Russia had lost during World War I. Stalin wanted to neutralize potential collaborators; the Crimean Tatars, a Muslim Turkic people, were prime suspects.

The Crimean Tatars' suffering goes as far back as 1783, when Russia first conquered and annexed the peninsula and began forcing them out. For hundreds of years before Russia took control, the Crimean Tatars had their own state, the Crimean Khanate.

Crimean Tatars still refuse to submit to Russian occupation. Most opposed the 2014 annexation, and their leadership continues to demand Crimea's reunification with Ukraine.

Russia has not taken kindly to this dissent. Russian authorities have shut down Crimean Tatar media. Russian forces have raided homes and mosques, and harassed and imprisoned Crimean Tatar activists, some of whom have disappeared or been killed. Russia has tried to block the Crimean Tatars from publicly commemorating the deportation and has even re-exiled Mustafa Dzhemilev, the Crimean Tatars' political leader.

According to Ukraine's Foreign Ministry, about 20,000 Crimean Tatars have fled the peninsula since the annexation. This is devastating for a people who spent 45 years banished from their homeland. Many thought they were done with Russia once and for all when the Soviet Union disintegrated and Crimea belonged to Ukraine. Few predicted that their nightmare would begin anew in 2014.

If the Crimean Tatars are to survive, Western governments must do more to help.

The first step is to formally recognize the Crimean Tatars as the indigenous people of Crimea. Ukraine finally did so two years ago, and the European Parliament later followed. Likewise, the 1944 deportation should be recognized as an act of genocide. Ukraine officially declared it so in 2015 and is now calling on other governments and organizations, including the United Nations, to do the same.

The State Department has issued the occasional news release denouncing Russia's treatment of the Tatars, but this is not enough.

After Russia's invasion of Crimea, President Obama signed executive orders outlining the sanctions the United States would apply and the justifications for them. These should be updated to cite Russia's human rights violations against the Tatars. The United States should also push for European Union officials to renew sanctions against Russia when they expire at the end of July. Not doing so would signal to Mr. Putin that he can get away with trampling on Ukraine's sovereignty.

In addition, American elected officials should support the Stand for Ukraine bill, introduced in Congress in April. The law would affirm the United States' refusal to recognize Russia's annexation of Crimea. More significantly, it would prevent the president from lifting the sanctions listed in the executive orders until Crimea's status has been resolved with Ukraine's approval.

The Crimean Tatars are doing all they can to resist the destruction of their culture. Last year activists prevented food and power coming from Ukraine from entering the peninsula. The blockade caused blackouts but demonstrated how dependent Crimea was on the Ukrainian mainland. Mr. Dzhemilev and other Crimean Tatar leaders in Ukraine frequently meet with foreign leaders and appear in the news media. Crimean Tatar representatives are trying to make their case to the United Nations.

Is anyone listening? The world does not have a good track record when it comes to protecting indigenous peoples; it is often too eager to sacrifice them for political expediency.

There are those who say that Crimea is a lost cause — that Mr. Putin will never allow it to be returned to Ukraine because Russian ties to the peninsula run too deep. They forget that Crimea belonged to the Crimean Tatars first, long before the Russian Empire, the Soviet Union and Mr. Putin.

CHRISTINA M. PASCHYN, an instructor of journalism at Northwestern University in Qatar, is the director of the documentary film "A Struggle for Home: The Crimean Tatars."

The Past 50 Years of Israeli Occupation. And the Next.

OPINION | BY NATHAN THRALL | JUNE 2, 2017

JERUSALEM — Three months after the 1967 war, Israel's ruling Mapai Party held a discussion on the future of the newly conquered territories. Golda Meir, who would become Israel's leader a year and a half later, asked Prime Minister Levi Eshkol what he planned to do with the more than one million Arabs now living under Israeli rule.

"I get it," Mr. Eshkol jokingly replied. "You want the dowry, but you don't like the bride!" Mrs. Meir responded, "My soul yearns for the dowry, and to let someone else take the bride."

On this 50th anniversary of the war, it is clear that over the half-century that followed, Israel managed to fulfill Mrs. Meir's wish, keeping control of the land indefinitely without wedding itself to the inhabitants. This resilient and eminently sustainable arrangement, so often mischaracterized as a state of limbo assumed to be temporary, has stood on three main pillars: American backing, Palestinian weakness and Israeli indifference. Together, the three ensure that for the Israeli government, continuing its occupation is far less costly than the concessions required to end it.

Each pillar, in turn, draws support from a core myth promoted by leaders in American, Palestinian or Israeli society. For Americans, the myth that the occupation is unsustainable is a crucial element in maintaining and excusing the United States' financial and diplomatic abetting of it. From the halls of the State Department to editorials in major newspapers and the pronouncements of pro-peace organizations like J Street, Americans are told that Israel will have to choose, and very soon, to give Palestinians either citizenship or independence, and choose to either remain a democracy or become an apartheid state.

Yet none of these groups calls on the United States to force this supposedly imminent choice, no matter how many times Israel demonstrates that it prefers a different, far easier option — continued occupation — with no real consequences. The only real fallout from continued occupation are major increases in American financing of it, with Israel now receiving more military assistance from the United States than the rest of the world does combined. Mistaking finger-wagging for pressure, these groups spend far too much time on phrasing their criticism of settlements and occupation, and far too little asking what can be done about it.

What supports the fiction that Israel cannot continue subjugating the Palestinians — and therefore that the United States will not be complicit in several more decades of subjugation — is a seemingly endless parade of coming perils, each of which, it is claimed or hoped, will cause Israel to end its occupation in the near future.

Initially, the threat was of an attack by the Arab states. But that soon crumbled: Israel made a separate peace with the strongest one, Egypt; the Arabs proved incapable of defending even sovereign Lebanon from Israeli invasion; and in recent years, many Arab states have failed to uphold even their longstanding boycott of Israel.

Then there was the demographic threat of a Palestinian majority arising between the Jordan River and the Mediterranean. But official Israeli and Palestinian population statistics indicate that Jews have been a minority in the territory Israel controls for several years now, and with no repercussions: A majority of the world's nations still speak of undemocratic rule by a Jewish minority as a hypothetical future, not an unacceptable present.

Later came the threat of renewed Palestinian violence. But Israel, with the strongest army in the region, has repeatedly demonstrated that it can endure and outlast whatever bursts of resistance the divided and exhausted Palestinians can muster.

The next threats, too, came up empty. The rise of nominally pro-Palestinian powers like India and China has, to date, had no negative effect on Israel, which has strengthened ties with both countries. The Boycott, Divestment and Sanctions movement, though noisy on some

American campuses, has yet to make a dent in Israel's economy or its citizens' self-reported level of life satisfaction, among the highest in the world.

Advocacy among some Palestinian intellectuals and their allies for enfranchisement in a single state, the so-called one-state solution, has not been endorsed by a single Palestinian faction and is a long way from drawing majority support in the West Bank and Gaza. If the proposal ever gathered momentum, Israel could easily counter it by withdrawing from the West Bank, as it did from Gaza in 2005.

The latest, though surely not the last, in this list of threats is the prospect of political changes within America and its Jewish community. Israel has become a more partisan issue, and polls show a majority of Democrats in favor of some economic sanctions or other action against Israeli settlements. Among American Jews, a growing rate of intermarriage with gentiles is lessening attachment to Israel, and Jewish organizations are increasingly divided over support for the country. Despite such vexation, mainly among liberal Jews, surveys over nearly four decades have shown overall American backing for Israel over the Palestinians only increasing, and none of the hand-wringing has translated into changes in American policy.

For American politicians, electoral and campaign finance incentives still dictate a baseline of unconditional support for Israel. The United States has given more than $120 billion to the country since the occupation began, spent tens of billions of dollars backing pro-Israel regimes ruling over anti-Israel populations in Egypt and Jordan, and provided billions more to the Palestinian Authority on condition that it continue preventing attacks and protests against Israeli settlements. And those expenditures do not reckon the cost to American security interests of Arab and Muslim resentment toward the United States for enabling and bankrolling the oppression of Palestinians in Gaza and the West Bank.

For the most part, the Palestinians themselves have done much to support the status quo. The myth upheld by leaders of the Palestinian government is that cooperating with Israel's occupation — which, in fact, makes the occupation less costly, more invisible to Israelis and easier to sustain — will somehow bring it to an end. This will happen, the theory goes, either because Palestinian good behavior will generate pressure from the contented Israeli public or because Israel, once deprived of excuses, will be forced by the United States and the international community to grant Palestinians their independence.

This is the myth underlying the continued support of the Oslo arrangements long after they were set to expire in 1999. It was also the basis for the two-year plan of former Prime Minister Salam Fayyad to build the institutions of a Palestinian state, and for the 12 years of quiescence and close security cooperation with Israel under President Mahmoud Abbas in the West Bank.

A counterpart to this myth, propounded by Israeli officials and regurgitated by American policy makers, is that Israel will not make concessions if pressured but will do so if it is warmly embraced. The historical record demonstrates the opposite.

Severe pressure from the United States, including the threat of economic sanctions, forced Israel to evacuate Sinai and Gaza after the 1956 Suez crisis. It also compelled Israel to commit to a partial Sinai pullout in 1975. It made Israel acquiesce to the principle of its withdrawal from territories occupied in the 1967 war, including the West Bank, in the 1978 Camp David accords. And it obliged Israel to reverse its incursions into southern Lebanon in 1977 and 1978.

By the same token, it was Palestinian pressure, including mass demonstrations and violence, that precipitated every Israeli withdrawal from Palestinian territory. Prime Minister Yitzhak Rabin, who agreed to the first Israeli pullouts from parts of the West Bank and Gaza, made his initial proposals for Palestinian self-government in 1989, when he was the defense minister attempting to quash the first intifada. Even Yitzhak Shamir, then the prime minister and a vehement opponent of ceding territory to the Arabs, put forward an autonomy plan for Palestinians later that year.

As the intifada developed into an increasingly militarized conflict in 1993, and Israel sealed off the occupied territories in March that year, Israeli negotiators held secret meetings with Palestinians near Oslo. There, they asked for an end to the intifada and soon agreed to evacuate the military government and establish Palestinian self-rule. In 1996, the clashes and riots known as the tunnel uprising led directly to Prime Minister Benjamin Netanyahu's promise to negotiate a withdrawal from most of Hebron, which Israel formally committed to do several months later.

During the second intifada, rocket attacks from Gaza increased sevenfold in the year before Prime Minister Ariel Sharon announced Israel would evacuate. (According to Israel's talking point, the army pulled out and got rockets; in fact, it was already getting rockets before it pulled out.) Shortly after the Gaza disengagement and the close of the intifada, a plurality of Israelis voted for the Kadima Party, led by the acting prime minister, Ehud Olmert, who ran on a platform of withdrawing from the roughly 91 percent of the West Bank that lies east of the separation barrier.

As bloodshed diminished, though, Israel's sense of urgency about the Palestinian problem dissipated. No serious proposals for unilateral withdrawal were made again until the level of violence in the West Bank and Jerusalem escalated in late 2015.

Finally, for Israel, the most pervasive myth is that there is no Palestinian partner for peace. Palestinians are irredeemably rejectionist, runs this argument; they will not give up on their impossible goals and have never made real compromises, in spite of every generous Israeli proposal. The truth is that the history of the Palestinian national movement is one long series of military defeats and ideological concessions. Each of those slowly moved the Palestine Liberation Organization from rejection of any Israeli presence to acceptance and recognition of Israel on the pre-1967 lines, compromising 78 percent of historic Palestine. For years, the international community bullied and cajoled the P.L.O. to accept a Palestinian state in the West Bank and Gaza, the remaining 22 percent.

When the P.L.O. finally did so, in 1988, the rug was pulled out from under it. Palestinians woke up to find that 22 percent of the homeland had been redefined as their new maximalist demand. Shimon Peres was among the few Israeli leaders to recognize the magnitude of the Palestinians' concession. He called it Israel's "greatest achievement."

In the last quarter-century of intermittent American-led negotiations, the powerlessness of the Palestinians has led to still further concessions. The P.L.O. has accepted that Israel would annex settlement blocs, consented to give up large parts of East Jerusalem, acknowledged that any agreement on the return of Palestinian refugees will satisfy Israel's demographic concerns and agreed to various limitations on the military capabilities and sovereignty of a future state of Palestine.

During that time, Palestinians were never presented with what Israel offered every neighboring country: full withdrawal from occupied territory. Egypt obtained sovereignty over the last inch of sand in Sinai. Jordan established peace based on the former international boundary, recovering 147 square miles. Syria received a 1998 proposal from Prime Minister Netanyahu (on which he subsequently backtracked) for a total evacuation from the Golan Heights. And Lebanon achieved a withdrawal to the United Nations-defined border without granting Israel recognition, peace or even a cease-fire agreement.

The Palestinians, though, remain too weak, politically and militarily, to secure such an offer, and the United States and the international community won't apply the pressure necessary to force Israel to make one. Instead, the United States and its allies pay lip service to the need to end the occupation, but do nothing to steer Israel from its preferred option of perpetuating it: enjoying the dowry, denying the bride.

NATHAN THRALL, a senior analyst at the International Crisis Group, is the author of "The Only Language They Understand: Forcing Compromise in Israel and Palestine."

In Kashmir, Blood and Grief in an Intimate War: 'These Bodies Are Our Assets'

BY JEFFREY GETTLEMAN | AUG. 1, 2018

QASBAYAR, KASHMIR — It was 9:30 p.m. when Sameer Tiger came to the door, a rifle slung over his shoulder.

Most of the village of Qasbayar, a tucked-away hamlet surrounded by apple orchards and framed by Kashmir's mountain peaks, was getting ready for sleep. A few yellowish lights burned in windows, but otherwise the village was dark.

"Is Bashir home?" Sameer Tiger asked. "Can we talk to him?"

Bashir Ahmad's family didn't know what to do. Mr. Ahmad wasn't a fighter; he was a 55-year-old pharmacist. And Sameer Tiger was a bit of mystery. He had grown up a skinny kid just down the road and used to lift weights with Mr. Ahmad's sons at the neighborhood gym; they'd spot each other with the barbells, all friends.

But Sameer Tiger had disappeared for a while and then resurfaced as a bushy-haired militant, a member of an outlawed Kashmiri separatist group that had killed many people, the vast majority of them fellow Kashmiris.

Kashmir's war, a territorial dispute between India and neighboring Pakistan, has smoldered for decades. Now it is collapsing into itself. The violence is becoming smaller, more intimate and harder to escape.

Years ago, Pakistan pushed thousands of militants across the border as a proxy army to wreak havoc in the Indian-controlled parts of Kashmir. Now, the resistance inside the Indian areas is overwhelmingly homegrown.

The conflict today is probably driven less by geopolitics than by internal Indian politics, which have increasingly taken an anti-Muslim direction. Most of the fighters are young men like Sameer Tiger from quiet brick-walled villages like Qasbayar, who draw support from a population deeply resentful of India's governing party and years of occupation.

Anyone even remotely associated with politics is in danger. That included Mr. Ahmad, who, when he wasn't sitting behind the counter of the village pharmacy, was known to host events for a local Kashmiri political party.

"Don't worry," Sameer Tiger said, standing at Mr. Ahmad's door, seeming to sense the family's anxiety.

He looked Mr. Ahmad's son right in the eye.

"We don't mean any harm," he said. "Your father is like our father."

Mr. Ahmad rushed home from work and invited Sameer Tiger in for tea. They sat on the living room carpet talking quietly, then Mr. Ahmad nodded goodbye to his wife and son and left with the visitor.

He didn't have much choice. Sameer Tiger was armed, and insistent, and had arrived with three others who were waiting in the road. The group moved slowly down the unlit lane.

At a bend in the road, in front of a shuttered shop, Sameer Tiger and Mr. Ahmad started arguing, a witness said. Four gun blasts rang out. Mr. Ahmad screamed. The few remaining lights in the neighborhood were suddenly extinguished.

JUST THE NAME KASHMIR conjures a set of very opposing images: snowy mountain peaks and chaotic protests, fields of wildflowers and endless deaths. It is a staggeringly beautiful place that lives up to all its fabled charm, yet even the quietest moments here feel ominous.

Kashmir sits on the frontier of India and Pakistan, and both countries have spilled rivers of blood over it. Three times, they have gone to war, and tens of thousands of people have been killed in the conflict. It is one of Asia's most dangerous flash points, where a million troops have squared off along the disputed border. Both sides now wield nuclear arms. And the two sides are divided by religion, with Kashmir stuck in the middle.

India, which has controlled most of the Kashmir Valley for the past 70 years, is predominantly Hindu. The valley itself is predominantly

A mosque in Srinagar. The Kashmir Valley is predominantly Muslim, but it is controlled by India, which is predominantly Hindu.

Muslim, as is Pakistan. But as the days pass, the conflict has become less of a religiously driven proxy war.

The rebellion, says Imran Khan, Pakistan's presumed new leader, is now "indigenous." Mr. Khan, who clearly has a Pakistani perspective on the conflict, says he is determined to negotiate an end to it. His persuasive election victory last month — and the fact that India's prime minister, Narendra Modi, made a friendly phone call to congratulate him — suggests a breakthrough is possible.

But India still loves to blame Pakistan for all its Kashmir problems, and Pakistan, according to Western intelligence agents, continues to send some money and weapons to militants in Kashmir. Many Indian politicians seem in denial that their own politics and policies might be a factor.

India's swerve to the right in recent years, with the rise of the Hindu nationalist Bharatiya Janata Party, has deeply alienated its

Muslim minority. Many top members of the ruling party have a very questionable record when it comes to treating Muslims fairly. This has emboldened Hindu supremacists across India, and in recent years, Hindu lynch mobs have targeted and killed Muslims, often based on false rumors. Many of the culprits are lightly punished, if at all, leaving India's Muslims feeling exposed.

In the Indian-administered parts of Kashmir, where there was already a history of bitter conflict, the new politics have spurred more people to turn against the government. Some pick up guns, others rocks, but the root emotion is the same: Many Kashmiris now hate India.

"This is what's different," said Siddiq Wahid, a Kashmiri historian who earned his Ph.D from Harvard. "Before, in the 1990s, many Kashmiris felt we can negotiate this, we can talk."

"But nobody wants to be part of India now," he said. "Every Kashmiri is resisting today, in different ways."

The latest are children and grandmothers. At almost every recent security operation, as Indian officers closed in on houses where militants were believed to be hiding, they have had to reckon with seething crowds of residents of all ages acting as human shields.

Walk through Kashmiri villages, where little apples are ripening on the trees and the air tastes clean and crisp, and ask people what they want. The most common response is independence. Some say they want to join Pakistan. None say anything good about India, at least not in public.

India's steely response has pushed away even moderates. Soldiers manhandle residents, cut off roads and barge into homes, saying they are looking for militants, who often hide among ordinary residents. When violent protests erupt, the Indian security services blast live ammunition and buckshot into the crowds, killing or blinding many people, including schoolchildren who are simply bystanders, despite cries from human rights groups to stop.

But while protests against Indian rule have grown in number and size, the armed militancy has become surprisingly small, partly because Pakistan is not providing as much support as it used to. Security officials say there are only around 250 armed militants operating in the Kashmir Valley, down from thousands two decades ago. Most of them are poorly trained and militarily lost. But still, the Indians can't stomp them out.

"I'll be honest," said Mohammad Aslam, a seemingly forthright police commander in southern Kashmir. "For every militant we kill, more are joining."

THE HUNT FOR SAMEER TIGER began the night he killed Mr. Ahmad, on April 15, 2017.

Back then, he wasn't widely known as Sameer Tiger. To most, he was still Sameer Bhat, a 17-year-old high school dropout who had worked in a local bakery. The Indian security forces give all the known militants a grade: A through C, with A being the most wanted. Sameer Tiger was a C.

The first place the police searched was Drabgam, his village. The shops are small, tucked into old brick buildings. The jobs are few. Like much of southern Kashmir, Drabgam hangs on the apple business. After the last of the apples have been picked in October and until the new crop is tended in the spring, there is little to do.

Sameer Tiger's house is one of the more modest: one and a half stories of crudely finished brick, a couple of naked electrical bulbs dangling in the living room, some wet shawls flapping on a line outside. His father is a laborer and farmer who tends just a few acres of orchards. His mother, Gulshan, is chatty and welcoming. They live on a dirt road.

"Sameer loves these," she said, pressing a handful of coconut candies into my palm and tugging me into their bare living room. The candies were exceptionally sweet and left a milky taste on the tongue.

Sameer Tiger's parents said their son was a reluctant militant. One afternoon in early 2016, he was accused of throwing rocks at police officers. Sameer Tiger was working in the bakery at the time, his parents said, and they insisted he was innocent.

But the police didn't listen and dragged him into a truck by his hair, they said. He spent a few days in jail. After he was let out, he disappeared.

Soon his face popped up on separatist websites, his piercing eyes staring at the camera, his bushy hair now down to his shoulders, a Kalashnikov in his hands.

"When we saw that," said Maqbool, his father, "we said goodbye."

More than 250,000 Indian Army soldiers, border guards, police officers and police reservists are stationed in the valley, outnumbering the militants 1,000 to one. Most militants don't last two years. One fighter, a former college sociology professor, was killed in May just two days after he joined.

Their attacks tend to be quixotic and they usually die in a hail of automatic weapon fire. Their assassinations and killings are not militarily significant, more acts of protest against Indian rule. Of the approximately 250 known militants, police officials said, only 50 or so came from Pakistan, and most of the rest, the locals, have never left the valley.

Sameer Tiger's parents said he changed his last name from Bhat to Tiger in honor of a brawny uncle with that nickname who was known for his immense strength.

When I asked about the killing of Bashir Ahmad, his father looked down at the carpet. For the first time, he seemed embarrassed about his son.

"Bashir was a good man," he mumbled. "Sameer wasn't there to kill him. It was an accident."

It might have been. On this point, Sameer Tiger's family and a survivor of the shooting seem to agree.

The night Mr. Ahmad was killed, the militants had also pulled another village elder from his home, Mohamad Altaf, a first cousin of Mr. Ahmad. Both were among Qasbayar's elite, landowners who supported the Peoples Democratic Party, Kashmir's dominant political organization.

The party used to sympathize with separatism, but to win control of the state parliament, it joined hands with the Hindu-nationalist Bharatiya Janata Party three years ago. Many Kashmiris accused it of selling out to Indian rule.

In June, the alliance suddenly broke apart, leaving a vacuum in the State Assembly. India's central government took over running the state. Kashmiris are now terrified that the government will escalate military operations; the sense of hopelessness is rising.

According to Mr. Altaf, as they walked through the unlit lanes of Qasbayar with the militants, Sameer Tiger urged him and Mr. Ahmad to renounce their party affiliation. When Mr. Ahmad started arguing, Sameer Tiger ordered both men to lie facedown and close their eyes.

Mr. Altaf was shot once in the back of his right knee and not critically hurt. He thinks the intent was to send a message.

But Mr. Ahmad was shot three times in his legs, the bullets moving upward toward his waist, Mr. Altaf said. His cousin, a lifelong friend, bled to death on the spot. Maybe the Kalashnikov jumped in Sameer Tiger's hands. Maybe he squeezed a split second too long. Mr. Altaf can't stop thinking about it. The betrayal haunts him.

"Bashir invited Sameer Tiger in for tea, *tea*," he said.

His cousin's death seems so pointless. He wonders if Sameer Tiger didn't set out that night to kill. Maybe, Mr. Altaf thinks, he just didn't know how to use his gun.

These days, the Kashmiri militants don't have many opportunities to practice shooting, police officials said. It is not like the 1990s, when thousands of young Kashmiri men slipped across the border to training camps on the Pakistani side. The Indians have sealed much of the contested frontier, which runs about 450 miles.

The Israelis have been surreptitiously helping them, providing security cameras, night vision gear, drones and other surveillance equipment along the border to stop big infiltrations. All this, coupled with the fact that Pakistan has closed most of its militant camps under pressure from the United States, has pushed the fighting away from the border, and deeper into the villages.

Kashmiris speak of a psychological tension that divides communities, individual families and sometimes even the same person. On one hand, people want to support a functioning society — to have their children go to school, get jobs, see some economic development — and

Mohamad Altaf, center, and his wife, Fareeda Akhtar, at home. Mr. Altaf was shot once in the back of his right knee by Sameer Tiger.

Indian control represents that. On the other, they feel real sympathy for a cause, Kashmiri independence, that they consider just.

"Let's be realistic: India's never going to give up this land," said one young Kashmiri who asked that his identity not be revealed because he could be labeled a collaborator.

"I can say such things in my house. But as soon as I step outside, even into my own street, I can't say that. It has to be 'Azadi! Azadi! Azadi!' " he said, using the word for freedom. "It's like you have to be two different people, all the time."

He sighed. "It's exhausting."

THE BIGGEST CHALLENGE IN KILLING MILITANTS, Officer Ashiq Tak explained, isn't finding them.

"Information is coming in all the time," he said. "We know their friends, their girlfriends, which houses they're using.

"The trick," he said, "is laying the cordon."

Officer Tak is another example of how this war is shrinking. He grew up in Qasbayar, a couple of miles from Sameer Tiger. Mr. Ahmad was his mother's brother. This winter he found himself, as the commanding officer of a tactical police unit in southern Kashmir, hunting the man who killed his uncle.

Sameer Tiger was emerging as a militant's militant. He was increasingly active — and not just on social media.

He attacked police stations, he recruited new fighters and he supplied pistols to young men to carry out assassinations, Officer Tak said. The police often discovered where he was hiding, and set up their security cordons, but he was slippery.

"We almost had him," Officer Tak said in February. "But he escaped, dressed like a girl."

Officer Tak seemed dispirited by all the support for Sameer Tiger, and the fact that many Kashmiris consider police officers like himself to be traitors. Unlike soldiers in the Indian Army, which is recruited from across the country, police officers in the region come from within the state of Jammu and Kashmir, and dozens have been killed.

Many Kashmiris see them as collaborators and call them "Modi's dogs," a reference to India's prime minister, who rose to power as part of the Hindu right-wing movement.

Officer Tak said that Kashmiris had so little faith in the security services that when a police officer or soldier killed a civilian, people didn't even bother demanding justice.

"Anywhere else, they'd ask for an investigation," he said. "Here, they just take the body and go away."

"That's a bad sign," he said. "That's total alienation."

SAMEER TIGER RESURFACED in late April, a year after Mr. Ahmad's death. A few miles from his house, witnesses said, he stopped a car carrying a local politician and shot him dead. The attack, conducted in the daytime and on a busy road, was unusually audacious. India's national news media seized upon it, and for the first time Sameer Tiger was front-page news.

The hunt for him intensified but more civilians were rallying to the defense of militants, often barricading the roads as the police closed in and pelting officers with rocks.

"It's getting very hard to do operations," Officer Tak grumbled.

Around this time a mysterious video appeared on Facebook in which Sameer Tiger issued a threat to Maj. Rohit Shukla, one of the area's commanding army officers: "Tell Shukla to come and face me."

A few days later, on April 30, the army got a tip that Sameer Tiger was hiding in a house in the center of Drabgam. Though he was now a highly wanted militant, upgraded to an A rating, it seemed he had never strayed far from home.

This time, the Indian Army didn't arrive en masse. They used mud-smeared dump trucks packed with soldiers wearing traditional pheran cloaks, guns hidden. The villagers thought they were laborers. The soldiers quietly surrounded the house and called for backup.

The soldiers sent in two rounds of emissaries, including village elders, to persuade Sameer Tiger to surrender. He replied with a burst of bullets, hitting Major Shukla in the shoulder.

The sound of gunfire served as an alarm, setting off an eruption. The village mobilized. Boys, girls, men and women scampered out of their houses and rushed into the road with stones in their hands. Mosque loudspeakers blared: "Sameer Tiger is trapped! Go help him!" The whole town, quite openly, was rallying to an outlaw's side.

As additional army trucks rumbled in, packed with troops, more civilians rushed forward, trying to insert themselves between the troops and Sameer Tiger. One young man was shot dead; the crowd kept coming.

But the cordon had been well laid, growing to nearly 300 soldiers and police officers. The civilians, however determined, couldn't break it.

Several police commanders said security officers then moved in, firing a rocket at the house. Flames burst out. Sameer Tiger scampered onto a rooftop. The soldiers opened up with automatic weapons from four directions. He was hit several times.

A CULTURE OF DEATH IS SPREADING across Kashmir. The militants have become the biggest heroes. People paint their names on walls. They wear T-shirts showing their bearded faces. They speak of them affectionately, as if they are close friends. The militants are especially revered after they are dead.

On a Tuesday morning, May 1, Sameer Tiger's lifeless body, riddled with holes and soaked in blood, was hoisted onto a makeshift wooden platform in the yard of one of Drabgam's mosques. Thousands poured in from across the valley. For hours they chanted his name: "Tiger! Tiger! Sameer Tiger!"

Boys scrambled up trees and scurried across tin roofs, the light metal popping beneath their gym shoes, to find any vantage point. Others fought through the nearly impenetrable crowd to the funeral pyre, just to gently stroke Sameer Tiger's beard or to kiss his pale face goodbye. Many vowed to join the militants.

One woman who identified herself as a separatist leader looked out at the sea of mourners and gravely smiled.

"We are winning," she said. "These bodies are our assets."

A few hundred yards away, on the rooftop where Sameer Tiger had been cornered, a team of boys wearing religious skullcaps scrubbed a rust-colored splotch. A crowd pressed in to watch.

"Young ones, tell me: What does the spilling of this blood mean?" one man shouted.

"*Azadi!*" the crowd roared back.

The boys worked fast, heads down, sweat trickling off their temples. They used wet rags to mop up the splotch. They squeezed the blood-water mixture into a copper urn, to be saved. An imam watching closely told them to capture every last drop of blood.

HARI KUMAR and **SAMEER YASIR** contributed reporting.

CHAPTER 6

Remembering and Reckoning With the Aftermath

After a war ends, it continues to have an impact on survivors for decades. People who survive conflicts as either
soldiers or civilians have always grappled with what we
now call post-traumatic stress disorder. On a larger scale,
institutions emerge to take the steps needed for healing: by fact-finding, bringing war criminals to justice and
seeking reconciliation. Such institutions, imperfect and
fragile, have become essential to a just resolution. The
persistence of such efforts depends on a final component:
the obligation to preserve the memory of what happened.

For Veterans, a Surge of New Treatments for Trauma

OPINION | BY TINA ROSENBERG | SEPT. 26, 2012

SUICIDE IS NOW the leading cause of death in the army. More soldiers die
by suicide than in combat or vehicle accidents, and rates are rising:
July, with 38 suicides among active duty and reserve soldiers, was the
worst month since the Army began counting. General Lloyd Austin
III, the army's second in command, called suicide "the worst enemy
I have faced in my 37 years in the army." This Thursday, the Army is
calling a "Suicide Stand-Down." All units will devote the day to suicide prevention.

There are many reasons a soldier will take his own life, but one major factor is post-traumatic stress.

Anyone who undergoes trauma can experience post-traumatic stress disorder — victims of rape and other crimes, family violence, a car accident. It is epidemic, however, among soldiers, especially those who see combat. People with PTSD re-experience their trauma over and over, with nightmares or flashbacks. They are hyperaroused: the slam of a car door at home can suddenly send their minds back to Iraq. And they limit their lives by avoiding things that can bring on the anxiety — driving, for instance, or being in a crowd.

PTSD has affected soldiers since war began, but the Vietnam War was the first in which the American military started to see it as a brain injury rather than a sign of cowardice or shirking. A study of Vietnam vets 20 years after the conflict found that a quarter of vets who served in Vietnam still had full or partial PTSD.

America's current wars may create even more suffering for those who fought them. In the Afghanistan and Iraq conflicts soldiers have been returned to these wars again and again, and they face a deadly new weapon — improvised explosive devices, or I.E.D.'s — which cause brain injuries that, terrible in themselves, also seem to intensify PTSD. "We surmise PTSD will be worse," said Dr. James Kelly, the director of the National Intrepid Center of Excellence, which studies and treats the intersection of PTSD and traumatic brain injury. "Some people are on their 10th deployment. Previously, people didn't have those doses. And there are multiple blast exposures and other blunt blows to the head. This kind of thing is new to us."

When we think about treating PTSD, we usually picture a single patient and a psychotherapist. The two treatments in widest use are, in fact, just that: cognitive processing therapy, where patients learn to think about their experiences in a different way, and prolonged exposure, in which the therapist guides the patient through re-experiencing his trauma again and again, to teach the brain to process it differently.

These therapies help a lot of veterans — about 40 percent of those who go through treatment are cured. But there are many, many more suffering veterans who are not helped. It's not just that these treatments don't work for everyone — no therapy does. More important, they are not broad enough. PTSD is often accompanied by and entwined with other serious problems — depression, sleep disorders, chronic pain and substance abuse. Sometimes these resolve if the PTSD does, but often they require specific attention — which the standard PTSD therapies don't provide.

There is another way these treatments need broadening — they need to reach more people. The military and Veterans Affairs hospitals do not have enough psychotherapists to offer them on the necessary scale. And many soldiers are wary of psychotherapy and afraid of the stigma it carries.

Today, the military is fighting that stigma. The V.A. is trying to integrate mental health care into primary health care; soldiers are now routinely screened for issues like PTSD, depression or substance abuse. A public awareness campaign called AboutFace features dozens of vets talking about their PTSD and how they got better — the point is: they are people just like you. A new program called Comprehensive Soldier and Family Fitness builds in resilience training for all soldiers at every phase — pre-deployment, in theater, upon return. It seeks to make regular mental health exercises as routine for soldiers as physical training.

According to a recent report by the National Academy of Sciences' Institute of Medicine, since 2005, the Pentagon and the V.A. have greatly increased funding for PTSD research. The V.A. has added 7,500 full-time mental health staff members and trained 6,600 clinicians to do cognitive processing and prolonged exposure therapies. Starting in 2008, all large V.A. clinics were required to have mental health providers onsite. The V.A. also added more centers that offer free, confidential counseling. Mobile centers bring counselors (themselves combat vets) to rural areas where other counseling is scarce.

All this effort however, is falling short. Only about 10 percent of those getting mental health care in the V.A. system are veterans of Iraq or Afghanistan — a vast majority of those treated are still Vietnam veterans. But some 2.4 million soldiers have been through Iraq and Afghanistan. The RAND Corporation's Center for Military Health Policy Research did a telephone survey of vets from these conflicts and found that one-third were currently affected by PTSD or depression or report exposure to a traumatic brain injury — and about 5 percent had all three. RAND also found that only half of those who reported symptoms of major depression or PTSD had sought any treatment in the past year.

Individual therapy is not the only way to treat PTSD. In January, a young man with the nickname of Trin (he asked that his real name not be published) sat down in a small, drab, room at a Veterans Affairs clinic in New Orleans with nine other men. All were veterans — of Iraq, Afghanistan, Operation Desert Storm or Vietnam; Trin had served in Iraq. All had PTSD. The men took chairs facing each other around tables pushed into a square, along with two women, who were running the group.

The facilitators asked everyone to do three drawings: of how they felt, where they were and where they wanted to be. Trin drew himself with no facial features. The next week, the facilitators put on some music and everyone stood up, faced a wall, and bounced to it. At other sessions they took large sheets of paper and colored in their family trees, with different colors for divorces, early deaths, conflicted relationships. And at almost every meeting over 10 weeks, they practiced conscious breathing and mindfulness.

"When they asked us to draw and color, people were rolling their eyes," Trin said. "We had older gentlemen, and some people might have thought this is kind of soft — not my lane."

Trin was anxious, cold and short-tempered. He was drinking a lot. Before starting this group, Trin had tried individual therapy, with no success. "My psychiatrist would ask a question and I would answer it," he said. "It was like talking to a wall. He didn't understand what I had gone through." He gave Trin a prescription for an anti-anxiety drug, which helped a little.

When Trin heard about the group, he quickly volunteered. By session five — the midpoint — he was sure it was helping. His sleep improved. The breathing exercises were things he could use to calm down. And having the group itself helped — men who had been through what he had gone through. On the last day, the group passed around stones — one for each participant. When your stone was passed around, each group member had to say something nice about you. "We put all that energy and kindness into each stone," said Trin. He carries his in his pocket.

Trin's program is a 10-week course designed by the Washington-based Center for Mind-Body Medicine. It is one of perhaps half a dozen different kinds of alternative therapies being tried for PTSD in military and V.A. hospitals.

You name it, and it's being used somewhere in the veterans' health system: The National Intrepid Center in Washington is one of many places using acupuncture to treat stress-related anxiety and sleep disorders; it has been shown to be effective against PTSD. At the New Orleans V.A., the same clinicians who ran Trin's group also did a small study using yoga. They found vets liked it and attendance was excellent. The yoga reduced the veterans' hyperarousal and helped them sleep. There is even a group in the Puget Sound V.A. Hospital in Seattle that treats PTSD — including among Navy Seals — using the Buddhist practice of "loving kindness meditation." ("We had a little bit of debate about changing the name," said Dr. David Kearney, who led the group. "But we decided to keep it, and it worked out just fine.")

One of the most promising techniques is mindfulness, inspired by Buddhist teaching, which emphasizes awareness of the present moment in order to choose how to respond to thoughts, feelings and events. Dr. Amishi Jha at the University of Miami is working with the military to develop mindfulness-based training for soldiers before they deploy, and Dr. Kearney has done a very small study of the effect of mindfulness on PTSD.

The Center for Mind-Body Medicine's program — the one Trin did — is the most comprehensive of all of them, giving participants a variety of different strategies to choose from: breathing, meditation, guided visual imagery, bio-feedback, self-awareness, dance, self-expression, drawing. And it is the one with the strongest evidence that it works to cure PTSD. In a trial in a Kosovo high school, students with PTSD who did the 10-week program had significantly greater reductions in PTSD than a control group of students assigned to wait for the course. Other before-and-after studies (with no control group) in Gaza have found an 80 to 90 percent reduction in PTSD with the technique, and those results still held months later. This is significantly better than any currently used individual therapy.

The Mind-Body program is in use at various V.A. hospitals, military bases, and at the National Intrepid Center. In some places it is studied, as well. At the Minneapolis V.A. Health Care System, for example, the psychologists Beret Skroch and Margaret Gavian found that in a Mind-Body group of patients with numerous problems, about 80 percent showed improvement.

Trin's group in New Orleans is part of the first randomized controlled trial measuring the program's effect on PTSD among U.S. veterans. Researchers are still measuring whether the results lasted two months after the last session, but Dr. James S. Gordon, the founder and director of The Center for Mind-Body Medicine, said that the patients' improvement at the last session was "at least as good" as the individual therapies the V.A. uses, with significantly lower dropout rates.

If those results hold up, then mind-body medicine is a potentially valuable addition to the V.A.'s limited menu of widely used therapies. It is built for large scale: psychotherapists are welcome but not necessary. Some of the groups are run by lay people; in Kosovo, high school teachers ran the groups. In Gaza, Center staff have trained 420 group leaders and worked with 50,000 people. Gordon said the center is currently capable of giving 10-day training and support for 1,500 group leaders a year.

Another advantage is that the program is broad-spectrum, showing success not only with PTSD, but depression, pain, sleep disorders and substance abuse. Dr. Barbara Marin, chief of addiction treatment services at Walter Reed National Military Medical Center, uses it there for patients with substance abuse problems. She calls it a "very effective" model.

Mind-body medicine and the other alternative therapies, moreover, may be more attractive to soldiers than the individual treatments, which have a 20 percent dropout rate. Both C.P.T. and prolonged exposure ask the patient to relive his trauma — an upsetting prospect for many soldiers. Some veterans avoid psychotherapy because they do not want to be singled out, judged and labeled deficient.

The alternative medicine groups, by contrast, have a dropout rate of virtually zero. Members can talk about their past trauma if they wish, but there is no pressure to do so. Instead, the groups are centered on the present, helping members to learn practical skills they can employ immediately. The facilitator does not sit in judgment — she's a participant in the group, sharing skills she might use herself for better sleep or stress reduction. Everyone, after all, can use help dealing with the stress of re-entry to civilian life. Going to a skills group instead of psychotherapy could remove much of the stigma of treatment.

Despite the vast increase in research money, studies of these skills groups have been small and isolated. Only randomized controlled trials are persuasive enough to get Washington to adopt a therapy on a wider scale, but these are too few and too slow, and starting new ones now would take years. It is time to take the most promising ideas and try them with thousands of people, not just a few dozen — and if they work, to expand them further. That is not cautious. But to continue with therapy as usual is to condemn hundreds of thousands of soldiers to a tour of duty without end.

TINA ROSENBERG won a Pulitzer Prize for her book "The Haunted Land: Facing Europe's Ghosts After Communism." She is a former editorial writer for The Times and the author of, most recently, "Join the Club: How Peer Pressure Can Transform the World" and the World War II spy story e-book "D for Deception."

Atoning for the Sins of Empire

OPINION | BY DAVID M. ANDERSON | JUNE 12, 2013

WARWICK, ENGLAND — The British do not torture. At least, that is what we in Britain have always liked to think. But not anymore. In a historic decision last week, the British government agreed to compensate 5,228 Kenyans who were tortured and abused while detained during the Mau Mau rebellion of the 1950s. Each claimant will receive around £2,670 (about $4,000).

The money is paltry. But the principle it establishes, and the history it rewrites, are both profound. This is the first historical claim for compensation that the British government has accepted. It has never before admitted to committing torture in any part of its former empire.

In recent years there has been a clamor for official apologies. In 2010, Britain formally apologized for its army's conduct in the infamous "Bloody Sunday" killings in Northern Ireland in 1972, and earlier this year Prime Minister David Cameron visited Amritsar, India, the site of a 1919 massacre, and expressed "regret for the loss of life."

The Kenyan case has been in process for a decade in London's High Court. The British fought to avoid paying reparations, so the decision to settle is a significant change of direction. The decision comes months ahead of the 50th anniversary of the British departure from Kenya — once thought of as the "white man's country" in East Africa.

The Kenya case turned on the evidence of historians, including my own role as an expert witness. I identified a large tranche of documents that the British government smuggled out of Kenya in 1963 and brought back to London. The judge ordered the release of this long-hidden "secret" cache, some 1,500 files.

The evidence of torture revealed in these documents was devastating. In the detention camps of colonial Kenya, a tough regime of physical and mental abuse of suspects was implemented from 1957 onward, as part of a government policy to induce detainees to obey orders or to make confessions.

The documents showed that responsibility for torture went right to the top — sanctioned by Kenya's governor, Evelyn Baring, and authorized at cabinet level in London by Alan Lennox-Boyd, then secretary of state for the colonies in Harold Macmillan's Conservative government.

When told that torture and abuse were routine in colonial prisons, Mr. Lennox-Boyd did not order that such practices be stopped, but instead took steps to place them beyond legal sanction. "Compelling force" was allowed, but defined so loosely as to permit virtually any kind of physical abuse.

Why did the British keep these documents, instead of destroying them? Plenty else was burned, or dumped at sea, as the British left Kenya.

The answer lay in the unease of some British colonial officers. Many did not like what they saw. When the orders to torture came down, some realized the jeopardy they were in. These men worried that it was they, not their commanders, who would carry the can.

They were right to worry. Official reports from the 1950s always blamed individual officers — the "bad apples in the barrel" — for acts of abuse. But the blame lay not with junior officers forced to implement a bad policy but with the senior echelons of a colonial government that was rotten to the core.

Kenya's will not be the last historical claims case. The Foreign and Commonwealth Office faces others, some of which have been in progress for years.

A case already before the courts concerns the 1948 Batang Kali massacre in colonial Malaya, now Malaysia. There, the relatives of innocent villagers — who were murdered by young conscript soldiers ordered to shoot by an older, psychopathic sergeant major — have asked for compensation. For Americans, the case has eerie echoes of Vietnam.

In Cyprus, translators employed by the British during the 1950s told tales of electrocutions and pulled fingernails as British intelligence officers tried to elicit information about gunrunning.

The case of Aden, now in Yemen, could be the worst of all. In 1965, the British governor retreated up the steps of his departing aircraft, firing his revolver at snipers arrayed around the airport runway. This was not the "orderly retreat from empire" that many historians would have us believe characterized British decolonization. Britain's brutality against its Yemeni enemies in Aden during those final days has become a local legend.

Though Britain is the first former European colonial power to pay individual compensation to victims, other countries have been confronted by similar accusations. In 2006, Germany offered to pay millions of euros to the Namibian government to compensate for the German Army's genocide against the Herero tribe in the early 20th century. It also issued a public apology in the capital, Windhoek. In 2011, the Dutch government was ordered by the International Court of Justice to compensate survivors of a 1947 massacre in colonial Indonesia; it has not yet paid.

Historical research has played its part in all these cases, but not all historians are happy with the way things are turning out. Leading historians of British colonialism have long tended to rejoice in a benevolent, liberal view of imperialism.

The British historians Andrew Roberts, Niall Ferguson and Max Hastings have all nailed their colors to the mast of the good ship Britannia as she sailed the ocean blue bringing civilization and prosperity to the world. This view seems unlikely to be credible for much longer.

Empire was built by conquest. It was violent. And decolonization was sometimes a bloody, brutal business. No American should need reminding of that. And Britain, along with other imperial powers of the 19th and 20th centuries, may yet have to pay for this.

Torture is torture, whoever the perpetrator, whoever the victim. Wrongs should be put right. Whatever wrongs were done in the name of Britain in Kenya in the 1950s, the British government has now delivered modest reparations to some victims. And maybe we in Britain have also finally begun to come to terms with our imperial past.

Would the United States be so accommodating to a similar claim? In the current political climate, probably not. But times change. Fifty years from now, will Americans face claims from Guantánamo survivors? You might, and perhaps you should.

DAVID M. ANDERSON, a professor of African history at the University of Warwick, is the author of "Histories of the Hanged: The Dirty War in Kenya and the End of Empire."

Khmer Rouge Tribunal: A U.N. Prosecutor's View

LETTER | THE NEW YORK TIMES | APRIL 13, 2017

TO THE EDITOR:

RE "KHMER ROUGE Tribunal's Record: 11 Years, $300 Million and 3 Convictions" (news analysis, April 11):

In deciding whether the Khmer Rouge tribunal was worth it, consider the magnitude of its task. Demographic studies estimate that at least 1.7 million people, almost a quarter of Cambodia's population, lost their lives under the Khmer Rouge. Millions more were forced to labor in cruel and inhumane conditions.

In June, the court will hear final arguments in the trial of Nuon Chea, No. 2 in the regime, and Khieu Samphan, a former head of state. By the number of victims, this is indisputably the biggest criminal trial since Nuremberg.

More than 236,000 people have attended the proceedings, and Cambodian newspapers covered testimony daily. Almost 4,000 victims are civil parties, this being the first international court where victims have this right.

The novel legal issues faced will set important precedents. The charges include forced marriage and rape related to the regime's policy to select spouses and require couples to consummate the marriage. The allegation of genocide against the Cham Muslim minority depends partly on evidence of the killing of those who refused to give up their religion.

How the court interprets the applicability of the Genocide Convention to these facts will establish a critical precedent for determining whether the ISIS campaign of forced conversion of Christians and Yazidis constitutes genocide.

We often hear world leaders respond to reports of atrocities in places like Syria by calling for those responsible to be held to account. For those promises to be credible, the international community cannot allow crimes of the magnitude of the Khmer Rouge to pass unaddressed.

NICHOLAS KOUMJIAN

PHNOM PENH, CAMBODIA

The writer is international co-prosecutor in the Extraordinary Chambers in the Courts of Cambodia, United Nations Assistance to the Khmer Rouge Trials.

How a Nation Reconciles After Genocide Killed Nearly a Million People

BY MEGAN SPECIA | APRIL 25, 2017

MBYO, RWANDA — They awoke early and gathered along a plot of land here in this Rwandan village made up of a handful of homes. Together, they began hacking away at a grass-bare patch with long-handled garden hoes. The mission: Dig a drainage ditch alongside a row of homes that had been continuously flooding during rains.

Scenes like this one were playing out across Rwanda on this Saturday — a monthly day of service known as Umuganda.

The premise is simple and extraordinary in its efficient enforcement: Every able-bodied Rwandan citizen between the ages of 18 and 65 must take part in community service for three hours once a month. The community identifies a new public works problem to tackle each month.

"We never had Umuganda before the genocide," said Jean Baptiste Kwizera, 21, wiping sweat from his brow as he took a break from the project here in Mbyo, about an hour's drive from Kigali, the capital.

Though the genocide ended a year before Mr. Kwizera was born, it is deeply ingrained in the lives of even the youngest Rwandans.

This compulsory work is emblematic of a broader culture of reconciliation, development and social control asserted by the government.

Each local umudugudu — or village — keeps track of who attends the monthly projects. Those who fail to participate without being excused risk fines and in some cases arrest.

Setting an example and seizing an opportunity to publicize the service on this Saturday, the country's president, Paul Kagame, helped break ground for a new elementary school in the country's northeast while dozens of photographers snapped photos.

"Umuganda is about the culture of working together and helping each other to build this country," Mr. Kagame told reporters.

Rwanda has been a unique experiment in national reconciliation and assiduously enforced social re-engineering in the more than two decades since its devastating genocide, when thousands in the country's Hutu ethnic majority unleashed unspeakable violence on the Tutsi minority and moderate Hutu countrymen who refused to take part in the slaughter. In just 100 days, nearly one million people perished.

Umuganda was revived and dozens of other nation-rebuilding exercises were conceived under Mr. Kagame, who came to power after the genocide and has held the presidency since 2000. A recent constitutional amendment paved the way for him to seek a third term in office, and in August he plans to do just that.

While many of his administration's programs have lowered poverty and child mortality rates, Mr. Kagame remains a controversial figure.

Many political analysts and human rights groups say Mr. Kagame has created a nation that is orderly but repressive. Laws banning so-called genocidal ideology that were adopted to deter a resurgence of sectarian or hate speech are also used to squelch even legitimate criticism of the government.

Against this backdrop, it is difficult to gauge sentiment about the effectiveness of reconciliation efforts, including Umuganda. The government's National Unity and Reconciliation Commission has twice released a "reconciliation barometer," which looks at dozens of factors to determine how well people are living together. In 2015, the last year for which the figures are available, the country deemed reconciliation in Rwanda was at 92.5 percent.

On this morning in Mbyo, none of the villagers openly questioned Umuganda or the wider reconciliation process.

"We needed security, and we found it because of our government," Mr. Kwizera said, praising a government he sees as essential for charting a path forward.

For the monthly day of service known as Umuganda, every able-bodied Rwandan between the ages of 18 and 65 must work on a designated project for three hours.

"I was in the part which was being hunted," he explained, describing his family's ethnic identity without ever saying the word Tutsi. Like others in this generation, who have been taught from their earliest school days to suppress any sense of ethnic identity, he considers himself simply Rwandan.

But in Mbyo, acknowledgment of past divisions is inescapable.

Mbyo is one of seven "reconciliation villages" established by Prison Fellowship Rwanda, a Christian organization that facilitates the small cluster of homes for those convicted of carrying out the violence and those who suffered at their hands.

Pastor Deo Gashagaza, who helped found the organization, created a process to connect Rwandans who had been imprisoned for participating in the slaughter with the families they harmed, and encourage dialogue through community-centered activities.

"Rebuilding the nation requires everyone to help," Mr. Gashagaza said. "We still have a lot of things to do for our communities, for social cohesion. It's painful, but it's a journey of healing."

In these villages, reconciliation is not just a moment. It is a way of life.

On a patch of property shaded by yellow flowering trees, Jacqueline Mukamana and Mathias Sendegeya sat side by side shelling peanuts and tossing them into a metal pan.

At first glance, the pair could be mistaken for husband and wife, leaning against each other with ease as they shucked the nuts. They were neighbors before the genocide and have known each other most of their lives, after growing up in a nearby village.

In 1994, Ms. Mukamana was 17. Her father, six brothers, five sisters and nine uncles were killed that April. She fled to Burundi. When she returned, her family home was destroyed.

Mr. Sendegeya was among the group that killed her father and four other members of her family, a fact that both speak about frankly but without much detail.

While Mr. Sendegeya takes responsibility for the murders, he believes that the political leaders of the past orchestrated the killings and that without that influence, his life would have been very different.

"That was the fault of the then government that pushed us to kill Tutsis," he said, his eyes gazing steadily ahead as he echoed a sentiment heard throughout the community from both perpetrators and survivors. "We massacred them, killed and ate their cows. I offended them gravely."

When he was in jail, he was waiting for death, and reconciliation never crossed his mind, he said.

Mr. Sendegeya re-entered society through a program that allows perpetrators to be released if they seek forgiveness from their victims. While in prison, he had reached out to Ms. Mukamana through Prison Fellowship Rwanda.

"He confessed and asked for forgiveness. He told me the truth," Ms. Mukamana explained. "We forgave him from our hearts. There is no problem between us."

But the healing process has taken years.

At first, Mr. Sendegeya feared for his safety. He thought that the genocide survivors living in Mbyo would kill him for what he had done. At the first community meeting that brought all of the residents together, he found it difficult to sit across from them, or even raise his eyes from the ground.

After moving to Mbyo, Ms. Mukamana had her own fears. She knew what the perpetrators had once been capable of, and imagined that Mr. Sendegeya would one day kill her.

Both said living in this facilitated community had allowed them the space to gradually come to a place of trust and forgiveness.

They are now raising a new generation of Rwandans. Mr. Sendegeya has a wife and nine children — six who were born before he went to prison and three who were born after he came back.

Ms. Mukamana and her husband have four children. She has taught them about the history of the genocide, and she said that they knew the role that Mr. Sendegeya had played in killing members of their family, but that they had never feared him.

"Our children have no problem among them," Mr. Sendegeya said.

Her children will go to his home to make meals, and she sometimes asks him to look after her children when she is away.

"This is the entrance of my home," Ms. Mukamana said, gesturing to her front door, steps away from where the pair sat together. "Whenever he encounters problems, he may call me and ask for help, and it is the same thing for me."

MEGAN SPECIA was a 2017 fellow with the International Women's Media Foundation's African Great Lakes Reporting Initiative.

Did America Commit War Crimes in Vietnam?

OPINION | BY CODY J. FOSTER | DEC. 1, 2017

ON DEC. 1, 1967, the last day of the International War Crimes Tribunal's second session, antiwar activists from around the world gathered in Roskilde, Denmark. The panel, also known as the Russell Tribunal after its founder, the philosopher Bertrand Russell, had spent a year investigating America's intervention in Southeast Asia and was now ready to announce its findings. Tribunal members unanimously found the United States "guilty on all charges, including genocide, the use of forbidden weapons, maltreatment and killing of prisoners, violence and forceful movement of prisoners" in Vietnam and its neighbors Laos and Cambodia.

Russell often stated that he was inspired by the Nuremberg trials. But the Russell Tribunal was not a government body or treaty organization; it had neither the legal authority nor the means to carry out justice after its findings. The tribunal's mission was to raise awareness about the impact of the war on Vietnamese civilians. "The Nuremberg Tribunal asked for and secured the punishment of individuals," Russell stated during the sessions. "The International War Crimes Tribunal is asking the peoples of the world, the masses, to take action to stop the crimes."

The philosopher Jean-Paul Sartre presided over the tribunal and helped to recruit 23 other internationally recognized academics, scientists, lawyers, former heads of state and peace activists whose self-professed moral consciousness persuaded them to accept the tribunal's invitation. Across two separate sessions, between May 2 and May 10, 1967, in Stockholm, and between Nov. 20 and Dec. 1, 1967 in Roskilde, the members weighed the evidence that each had found during several fact-finding trips to Vietnam between the two sessions.

These missions allowed tribunal members to assess the damage the war had wrought on civilians and verify firsthand the claims heard during the tribunal's first session. One such mission, which included the labor activist Lawrence Daly, the journalist Tariq Ali and the writer Carol Brightman, returned with indisputable proof that the United States Air Force had deliberately bombed civilian facilities and infrastructure, including hospitals, schools, churches and villages.

Other members who scouted the countryside encountered civilians who agreed to travel to Denmark and speak before the tribunal's second session. The first witness, a 37-year old Vietnamese farmer, exposed his charred body before the tribunal and explained through an interpreter that an American plane had dropped phosphorus bombs on his family farm in Quang Nam province in South Vietnam while he plowed the field.

He wasn't alone. Victim after victim described how American interrogators swept through villages, looking for the enemy and torturing civilians for information. One former American interrogator, Peter Martinsen, confirmed with the tribunal that the Army Intelligence School taught interrogation strategies that violated the Geneva Conventions. "Interrogators participated in actual torture," he said, before commenting on how those methods occasionally resulted in the death of Vietnamese prisoners of war. Later, in 1970, additional interrogators and Vietnamese people confirmed that they had been waterboarded, shocked and burned. A few even shared how they were sexually assaulted through the insertion of snakes and sticks into their bodies. "It's so horrifying to recall an interrogation where you beat the fellow to get an effect, and then you beat him out of anger, and then you beat him out of pleasure," Martinsen added.

Such testimony also revealed that the United States had forcefully relocated civilians to better isolate the enemy. The strategic hamlet program, for example, forced large populations of people into sanctioned districts in order to pacify rural villages and halt the communist infiltration into the countryside. Witnesses testified that American soldiers murdered resisters and burned villages as they relocated Vietnamese civilians. American bombers and artillery would then subject the reportedly empty village to bombs and artillery fire before covering the area with chemical defoliants. Such tactics eradicated countless livelihoods; most survivors had little choice but to abandon hope and move their families into the prepared hamlets.

Tribunal members were equally worried about the military's use of advanced weaponry in areas populated by civilians. One particular bomb gave them pause because its design seemed intent only on inflicting mass casualties. A weapons expert, Jean-Pierre Vigier of the University of Paris, testified before the tribunal that the so-called guava bomb — a type of cluster bomb — could send 300 iron balls of shrapnel in every direction upon explosion. The bomb did little damage to concrete and steel, he said; instead, it appeared as if it were created to tear through the flesh of human bodies. "I don't see any conclusion except that bombing the civilians is a deliberate policy of the Pentagon, presumably in hopes of inducing them to bring pressure on their government to surrender," Daly concluded upon hearing the testimony.

If only for a moment, the tribunal's findings helped invigorate the global antiwar movement to increase pressure on the Johnson administration to bring the Vietnam War to a close. Influenced by what they had already witnessed in Vietnam between the two sessions, two tribunal members, the antiwar activist Dave Dellinger and the writer Carl Oglesby, worked with antiwar activists to plan a peaceful protest to occur around the world in October 1967. That month tens of thousands of antiwar demonstrators faced off against troops outside the Pentagon and in front of American embassies across Western Europe, in Central and South America, and throughout Asia. Russell's Campaign for Nuclear Disarmament and the British Council for Peace in Vietnam organized demonstrations in Washington and outside 10 Downing Street in London. The Vietnam Solidarity Campaign, yet another organization sponsored by Russell, collaborated with Tariq Ali to stage a march in Trafalgar Square in addition to picketing outside the Australian, New Zealand and American embassies.

The tribunal and the marches did not bring the war to a close, but they helped energize international opposition to colonialism and imperialism: Puerto Rican nationalists who sought to liberate their country from American imperialism, for example, saw the Vietnamese as spiritual allies, even as Puerto Ricans were drafted to fight on behalf of the United States in Vietnam.

The tribunal resonated in the United States, too. Stokely Carmichael, a member of the tribunal, and other young black leaders joined hands with these revolutionaries as they came to see American war crimes in Vietnam as another product of the racially oppressive nature of American imperialism. They argued that the African-American community existed as an internal colony dominated by racial hatred and violence.

War crimes uncovered by the tribunal and, later, the My Lai massacre poisoned American credibility abroad and sparked a domestic national identity crisis. Such revelations forced American citizens to come to terms with the military's "kill anything that moves" approach to the war. And yet that reckoning didn't last; the reality of America's crimes in Vietnam has been blanketed over by presidents, politicians and other leaders looking to heal the country — even if that meant ignoring history — to promote a new patriotic nationalism. Government-backed corporate slogans such as "The Pride Is Back" campaign in the 1980s manipulated collective memory by overlooking the war crimes and human rights violations that the tribunal helped to expose.

The tribunal's most significant legacy was the appearance of "people's tribunals" long after the Vietnam War ended. People's courts, called "Russell Tribunals," have investigated Third World dictatorships, the 1973 Chilean coup, the Israeli-Palestinian conflict and the war in East Ukraine. Most recently, the World Tribunal on Iraq opened in 2003 to charge the United States with war crimes and violating the Geneva Conventions. Once again the tribunal forced the world to listen to new narratives of civilian bombing and new torture tactics adopted by American armed forces.

Russell's hope was that his tribunals would build momentum toward a people-driven, international peace movement that did more than protest. In his mind, the people — properly organized and motivated — could hold governments in check. It was an urgent idea in 1967; it remains one today.

CODY J. FOSTER is a doctoral candidate in history and a presidential fellow at the University of Kentucky.

Poland Digs Itself a Memory Hole

OPINION | BY MARCI SHORE | FEB. 4, 2018

"LIFE, AS WE find it, is too hard for us," Sigmund Freud wrote. "In order to bear it we cannot dispense with palliative measures."

Since coming to power in Poland in 2015, Law and Justice, the nationalist populist party led by Jaroslaw Kaczynski, has embarked on a series of palliative measures. The most recent is a draft law outlawing accusations of Polish participation in the Holocaust and other war crimes that took place during the German occupation of Poland. In the past 10 days, the bill has been approved by both legislative houses, the Sejm and the Senate. Poland's president, Andrzej Duda, was given 21 days to decide whether to sign the bill.

This draft law is part of a program introduced in the past two years, named by the Law and Justice government "a good change." The change has included attempts to legalize government control of the media and introduce draconian anti-abortion laws. Law and Justice has also debased public language, conjuring phrases reminiscent of the "newspeak" of the Communist years. Liberals have become "pigs cut off from the trough."

"Volksdeutsch" once referred to Poles who, during the Nazi occupation, betrayed Poland by registering as ethnic Germans to secure the occupier's favor. Now, "becoming a 'Volksdeutsch' " describes Polish citizens who ask the European Union to investigate the government's constitutional violations — for example, denying the force of law to decisions of the Constitutional Tribunal and passing laws that abolish an independent judiciary.

Communists once spoke of "enemies of the people." Today Mr. Kaczynski labels those who criticize the government "the worst sort of Poles." They are those who reject the "joyous mood" of authentic Poles, otherwise called Law and Justice supporters. The "worst kind" have taken to the streets to protest in larger numbers than Poland has seen since Solidarity.

To Mr. Kaczynski, these demonstrators have "trampled on all that is holy in our culture," in particular his vision of unblemished Polish heroism and martyrdom.

The government has purged cultural institutions of critical voices. For decades, Martin Pollack, the Austrian author and translator of Polish literature, has been indispensable in East-West dialogue. In 2011 he was awarded the Leipzig Book Prize for European Understanding. After publishing an essay criticizing Law and Justice in the Austrian newspaper Der Standard, he was blacklisted from the Polish Cultural Institute. The series of literary evenings with Polish authors Mr. Pollack had organized in Vienna was canceled.

In 2016, Law and Justice's minister of culture, Piotr Glinski, announced an intention to in effect liquidate the Gdansk Museum of the Second World War. By then the $120 million project had been eight years in the making; it opened in 2017. The museum has an international scope; the main exhibit begins with the collapse of the liberal order intended after World War I: Italian fascism, German Nazism, Polish authoritarianism, Soviet Stalinism, Japanese imperialism.

The Polish historian Anna Muller, who teaches at the University of Michigan-Dearborn, helped design the exhibits. She met with a Polish priest, Mikolaj Sklodowski, who was born in 1945 in the Ravensbrück concentration camp. He showed her a medallion of St. Nicholas that his mother hid in a bar of soap while in Ravensbrück. He gave it to her for the museum.

In 1938, 24-year-old Jakub Piekarz left the small town of Jedwabne in eastern Poland for the United States. Three years later, just after the Red Army had withdrawn and the Wehrmacht had invaded the town, Jedwabne's Jews, including Mr. Piekarz's parents, were murdered by their Polish neighbors. In 2000, the historian Jan Tomasz Gross published a book about the massacre; what followed was the most important debate on the Holocaust to take place in post-Communist Europe.

Mr. Piekarz (by then Rabbi Baker) died in 2006. In 2013 Ms. Muller visited his daughter in New York; she gave Ms. Muller her father's letters, photographs and the passport with which he had left Poland in 1938.

The museum now has over 13,000 donated artifacts like Father Sklodowski's medallion and Rabbi Baker's passport. The government believes that the museum insufficiently expresses "the Polish point of view." The museum's original director, Pawel Machewicz, has been dismissed.

For now, the original main exhibition remains, but the five-minute concluding film has been removed. The censored documentary moves chronologically from the Nuremberg trials through the Korean War, the Ku Klux Klan, Stalin's death, Martin Luther King's "I Have a Dream" speech, John F. Kennedy's assassination, the testing of an atomic bomb, the Polish "anti-Zionist" campaign of 1968, Nelson Mandela, Polish Solidarity, Ronald Reagan's meeting with Mikhail Gorbachev, Sept. 11, the Iraq war, the recent hell of Aleppo and refugees drowned in the Mediterranean. It is set to the music of "House of the Rising Sun."

It is not at all anti-Polish. It is cosmopolitan — and peculiarly devastating because it forces us to question what is particular and what is universal, which horrors we have left behind, and which remain with us.

The rejection of the universal — the insistence on Polish exceptionalism — is at the heart of Poland's "historical policy," which aims to control the narrative of the 20th century in such a way as to glorify and exonerate Poles. The underlying principles are simple: a trope of Christ-like martyrdom; a Manichaean division between innocence and guilt, and an assurance that everything bad came from outside.

It was the publication of Mr. Gross's "Neighbors" that motivated the first attempts, in 2006 during the first Law and Justice government, to enshrine historical policy by criminalizing the denial that Poles were innocent of any Nazi or Communist crimes. At that time, the Polish historian Dariusz Stola protested against the abdication of responsibility: "If neither groups of nor individual Polish citizens had anything to do with these crimes, then why all the ado about the iniquities of the Communist regime?" he asked. "After all, everything bad was done by some alien creatures, most likely Martians."

Several years ago, the Polish courts declared the original law unconstitutional on technical grounds. But on Jan. 26, the Sejm renewed the project, approving an article stipulating a punishment of up to three years in prison for those who "publicly and against the facts attribute to the Polish nation or the Polish state responsibility or co-responsibility for Nazi crimes committed by the German Third Reich" or for "other crimes against peace, humanity or war crimes."

The Polish Center for Holocaust Research responded: "We consider the adopted law a tool intended to facilitate the ideological manipulation and imposition of the history policy of the Polish state."

In this context (arguably not entirely unlike the present one in the United States), xenophobia — against Jews, Ukrainians, Muslims, Roma, L.G.B.T. people and others — is expressed with ever more impunity. Between 2015 and 2017, reported hate crimes increased 40 percent. In April 2016, the Council of Ministers liquidated the Council Against Racial Discrimination, Xenophobia and Related Intolerance created in 2013.

In May 2016 the Polish playwright Pawel Demirski was brutally beaten for defending a Pakistani man being harassed by soccer fans. In September, the historian Jerzy Kochanowski was riding on a tram in Warsaw with a visiting German colleague. A man approached Mr. Kochanowski and told him to stop speaking German. Mr. Kochanowski explained that his friend did not speak Polish. Then the man began to beat him. The tram driver declined to call the police; Professor Kochanowski ended up in the hospital with five stitches.

Last Nov. 11, Polish Independence Day, thousands of nationalists marched under the slogans "We want God" and "Poland only for Poles." Later, the Polish historian Marek Chodakiewicz, who has been among Mr. Gross's most vicious attackers, and who now occupies a chair of Polish studies at the Institute of World Politics in Washington, wrote that the so-called March of Independence "grew from the need to demonstrate our pride in the fact that we belong to a historical continuity, which is worthy of defending against threats emerging from liberalism and lefty-ism, including Marxism-lesbianism and multiculturalism." The Polish press reported that President Trump consulted Mr. Chodakiewicz in preparing the speech the president delivered last July in Warsaw.

(A week after the nationalists' march, a Polish journalist asked me how I felt watching the demonstrations. Very much like how I felt watching the white supremacists march in Charlottesville, I told him.)

In his book "Hitler's Willing Executioners," the American political scientist Daniel Goldhagen argued that Germans had for generations been infected with virulent anti-Semitism. They were bad people who enjoyed killing Jews. Mr. Goldhagen's greatest opponent from beyond the grave was Hannah Arendt. "For many years now," she wrote late in the war, "we have met Germans who declare that they are ashamed of being Germans. I have often felt tempted to answer that I am ashamed of being human."

In explaining Mr. Goldhagen's appeal, the Czech political theorist Pavel Barsa wrote, "if Goldhagen is right, then we can all sleep soundly."

Alas, because Arendt and Freud were right and Mr. Goldhagen was wrong, we can never sleep soundly again. Among Freud's unpleasant messages is this: What threatens us is never securely outside of ourselves. Historical policy — like nationalism more broadly, in Poland as elsewhere — serves as an evasion of responsibility, an attempt at psychic consolation through the exporting of guilt, a desire to find a safe place in the world.

MARCI SHORE is an associate professor of history at Yale and the author, most recently, of "The Ukrainian Night: An Intimate History of Revolution."

Glossary

antithetical Opposed to or the opposite of something.

asylum The protection granted by a country to a refugee from another country.

Blackwater A private military company founded by Erik Prince, utilized by the United States military during the Iraq occupation.

byzantine When something requires an unnecessary amount of bureaucratic detail.

civilian A citizen who is not a member of the armed forces.

counterinsurgency Military operations designed to contain or stop an uprising against an occupying force.

crime against humanity The systematic undertaking of a violent or destructive act against people on a large scale.

crown prince A designated male heir to a monarchy.

deterrent Acting to discourage a deed or event from taking place.

displaced persons camp A camp set up as a temporary shelter for people displaced during wartime.

drone An unmanned aircraft used to carry out surveillance or airstrikes against a military target.

emancipation The act of releasing an enslaved person.

embargo A legal restriction on trade or commerce with another country.

enhanced interrogation The official name for interrogation techniques used by the United States, later identified as forms of torture.

famine The widespread scarcity of food in a particular area.

Geneva Conventions A set of international treaties and protocols that govern the laws of war.

genocide Acts, including but not limited to mass killings, intended to exterminate members of a particular ethnic group.

imperialism A nation exerting military, political and economic power over other nations.

impunity Free of punishment or consequence for an action.

interventionism The doctrine of military involvement in overseas affairs.

ISIS Islamic State of Iraq and Syria, also known as Islamic State of Syria and the Levant, or Daesh. ISIS is an extremist Muslim theocracy that began conquering territory in the chaos of the Iraq war.

Nuremberg Trials The trials of Axis leaders following World War II, which set a model for future trials concerning war crimes.

occupation The military control of conquered enemy territory after a war.

palliative A solution that treats the symptoms but not the causes.

post-traumatic stress disorder Anxiety and other psychological symptoms following a traumatic event.

proxy war A war influenced or led by a country that is not itself involved.

realpolitik An approach to politics that claims to be motivated by circumstances rather than ideology.

refugee A person who flees a country to escape persecution or war.

war crime A violation of the laws of war, often relating to treatment of civilians or prisoners of war.

waterboarding An act of torture that simulates the experience of drowning in a victim.

Media Literacy Terms

"Media literacy" refers to the ability to access, understand, critically assess and create media. The following terms are important components of media literacy, and they will help you critically engage with the articles in this title.

angle The aspect of a news story that a journalist focuses on and develops.

attribution The method by which a source is identified or by which facts and information are assigned to the person who provided them.

balance Principle of journalism that both perspectives of an argument should be presented in a fair way.

bias A disposition of prejudice in favor of a certain idea, person or perspective.

byline Name of the writer, usually placed between the headline and the story.

chronological order Method of writing a story presenting the details of the story in the order in which they occurred.

credibility The quality of being trustworthy and believable, said of a journalistic source.

editorial Article of opinion or interpretation.

feature story Article designed to entertain as well as to inform.

headline Type, usually 18 point or larger, used to introduce a story.

human interest story Type of story that focuses on individuals and how events or issues affect their life, generally offering a sense of relatability to the reader.

impartiality Principle of journalism that a story should not reflect a journalist's bias and should contain balance.

intention The motive or reason behind something, such as the publication of a news story.

interview story Type of story in which the facts are gathered primarily by interviewing another person or persons.

inverted pyramid Method of writing a story using facts in order of importance, beginning with a lead and then gradually adding paragraphs in order of relevance from most interesting to least interesting.

motive The reason behind something, such as the publication of a news story or a source's perspective on an issue.

news story An article or style of expository writing that reports news, generally in a straightforward fashion and without editorial comment.

op-ed An opinion piece that reflects a prominent individual's opinion on a topic of interest.

paraphrase The summary of an individual's words, with attribution, rather than a direct quotation of their exact words.

quotation The use of an individual's exact words indicated by the use of quotation marks and proper attribution.

reliability The quality of being dependable and accurate, said of a journalistic source.

rhetorical device Technique in writing intending to persuade the reader or communicate a message from a certain perspective.

tone A manner of expression in writing or speech.

Media Literacy Questions

1. "Block the Sale of Warplanes to Nigeria" (on page 19) is an editorial. Comparing it with the news story "Sentences in Blackwater Killings Give Iraqis a Sense of Closure" (on page 16), what differences do you notice?

2. What is the angle of the article "At a 'Defense' Expo, an Antiseptic World of Weaponry" (on page 21)? Use the wording of the headline when forming your answer.

3. The news story "ISIS Committed Genocide Against Yazidis in Syria and Iraq, U.N. Panel Says" (on page 48) uses very specific sources. What sources are they, and why might they be especially relevant to reporting on the crime of genocide?

4. Kevin Rudd's article "Myanmar's Rohingya Crisis Meets Reality" (on page 60) has a specific motive. What is it? Use the headline, first paragraph and the article's angle to determine that motive.

5. "ISIS Enshrines a Theology of Rape" (on page 83) relies on many sources that choose to remain anonymous. How does the author use direct quotes and paraphrase to convey information while preserving the sources' safety?

6. "How U.S. Torture Left a Legacy of Damaged Minds" (on page 99) is a human interest story. How does the authors' descriptive language help readers understand the experience of former Guantánamo detainees?

7. Rick Gladstone's article "U.N., Fearing a Polio Epidemic in Syria, Moves to Vaccinate Millions of Children" (on page 125) is written in the inverted pyramid style. Comparing earlier and later paragraphs, what types of reporting seem to be most important for the story?

8. What is the intention of the article "The Tragedy of Saudi Arabia's War" (on page 136)? In forming your answer, consider the photography subjects and repeated references to the Saudi coalition.

9. Christina M. Paschyn's article "Russia Is Trying to Wipe Out Crimea's Tatars" (on page 163) is an op-ed. Based on the bio at the end of the article, what features of Paschyn's background best qualify her perspective?

10. "In Kashmir, Blood and Grief in an Intimate War: 'These Bodies Are Our Assets' " (on page 173) relies on a number of sources, including militants, their families and military police. Based on the motives of each source, what bias might impact each source's credibility? How does the author report each source?

11. "Did America Commit War Crimes in Vietnam?" (on page 202) is written in chronological order. How does this order help readers understand the described tribunal and its immediate effects?

12. "Poland Digs Itself a Memory Hole" (on page 207) begins with an older quotation from Sigmund Freud. What is the purpose of this rhetorical device? How does it contribute to the author's argument about remembering wartime atrocities?

Citations

All citations in this list are formatted according to the Modern Language Association's (MLA) style guide.

BOOK CITATION

THE NEW YORK TIMES EDITORIAL STAFF. *Casualties of War*. New York: New York Times Educational Publishing, 2020.

ONLINE ARTICLE CITATIONS

ANDERSON, DAVID M. "Atoning for the Sins of Empire." *The New York Times*, 12 June 2013, https://www.nytimes.com/2013/06/13/opinion/atoning-for -the-sins-of-empire.html.

APUZZO, MATT, ET AL. "How U.S. Torture Left a Legacy of Damaged Minds." *The New York Times*, 8 Oct. 2016, https://www.nytimes.com/2016/10/09 /world/cia-torture-guantanamo-bay.html.

BARNARD, ANNE, ET AL. "As Atrocities Mount in Syria, Justice Seems Out of Reach." *The New York Times*, 15 Apr. 2017, https://www.nytimes.com /2017/04/15/world/middleeast/syria-bashar-al-assad-evidence.html.

BEECH, HANNAH. "Myanmar's Military Planned Rohingya Genocide, Rights Group Says." *The New York Times*, 19 July 2018, https://www.nytimes .com/2018/07/19/world/asia/myanmar-rohingya-genocide.html.

CALLIMACHI, RUKMINI. "ISIS Enshrines a Theology of Rape." *The New York Times*, 13 Aug. 2015, https://www.nytimes.com/2015/08/14/world /middleeast/isis-enshrines-a-theology-of-rape.html.

CHOKSHI, NIRAJ, AND MATTHEW HAAG. "Why Ilhan Omar and Elliott Abrams Tangled Over U.S. Foreign Policy." *The New York Times*, 14 Feb. 2019, https://www.nytimes.com/2019/02/14/us/politics/ilhan-omar-elliott -abrams.html.

CUMMING-BRUCE, NICK. "ISIS Committed Genocide Against Yazidis in Syria and Iraq, U.N. Panel Says." *The New York Times*, 16 June 2016, https://www

.nytimes.com/2016/06/17/world/middleeast/isis-genocide-yazidi-un.html.

CUMMING-BRUCE, NICK. "U.N. Official Condemns Use of Torture in Syrian War." *The New York Times*, 14 Apr. 2014, https://www.nytimes.com /2014/04/15/world/middleeast/torture-in-syria.html.

DEBRABANDER, FIRMIN. "Drones and the Democracy Disconnect." *The New York Times*, 14 Sept. 2014, https://opinionator.blogs.nytimes.com/2014/09 /14/drones-and-the-democracy-disconnect/.

FOSTER, CODY J. "Did America Commit War Crimes in Vietnam?" *The New York Times*, 1 Dec. 2017, https://www.nytimes.com/2017/12/01/opinion /did-america-commit-war-crimes-in-vietnam.html.

GLADSTONE, RICK. "Cholera, Lurking Symptom of Yemen's War, Appears to Make Roaring Comeback." *The New York Times*, 27 Mar. 2019, https:// www.nytimes.com/2019/03/27/world/middleeast/cholera-yemen.html.

GLADSTONE, RICK. "U.N., Fearing a Polio Epidemic in Syria, Moves to Vaccinate Millions of Children." *The New York Times*, 25 Oct. 2013, https://www .nytimes.com/2013/10/26/world/middleeast/syria-polio-epidemic.html.

GETTLEMAN, JEFFREY. "Drought and War Heighten Threat of Not Just 1 Famine, but 4." *The New York Times*, 27 Mar. 2017, https://www.nytimes .com/2017/03/27/world/africa/famine-somalia-nigeria-south-sudan -yemen-water.html.

GETTLEMAN, JEFFREY. "In Kashmir, Blood and Grief in an Intimate War: 'These Bodies Are Our Assets.' " *The New York Times*, 1 Aug. 2018, https:// www.nytimes.com/2018/08/01/world/asia/kashmir-war-india-pakistan .html.

HUBBARD, BEN. "At a 'Defense' Expo, an Antiseptic World of Weaponry." *The New York Times*, 23 Feb. 2017, https://www.nytimes.com/2017/02/23/world /middleeast/weapons-defense-expo-abu-dhabi.html.

IBRAHIM, MOHAMED, AND JEFFREY GETTLEMAN. "Ethiopian Army Begins Leaving Mogadishu." *The New York Times*, 2 Jan. 2009, https://www .nytimes.com/2009/01/03/world/africa/03somalia.html.

JAWOSHY, OMAR AL-, AND TIM ARANGO. "Sentences in Blackwater Killings Give Iraqis a Sense of Closure." *The New York Times*, 14 Apr. 2015, https:// www.nytimes.com/2015/04/15/world/middleeast/sentences-in-blackwater -killings-give-iraqis-a-measure-of-closure.html.

KAHN, JOSEPH. "Officials Fear Tuberculosis Epidemic in Camps." *The New York Times*, 22 Oct. 2001, https://www.nytimes.com/2001/10/22/world/a -nation-challenged-health-officials-fear-tuberculosis-epidemic-in-camps.html.

MCKINLEY, JAMES C., JR. "Deadly Epidemic Emerges in Sudan." *The New York Times*, 18 July 1997, https://www.nytimes.com/1997/07/18/world /deadly-epidemic-emerges-in-sudan.html.

THE NEW YORK TIMES. "Block the Sale of Warplanes to Nigeria." *The New York Times*, 18 May 2016, https://www.nytimes.com/2016/05/18/opinion /block-the-sale-of-warplanes-to-nigeria.html.

THE NEW YORK TIMES. "Famine Stalks South Sudan." *The New York Times*, 6 Mar. 2018, https://www.nytimes.com/2018/03/06/opinion/famine -stalks-south-sudan.html.

THE NEW YORK TIMES. "Khmer Rouge Tribunal: A U.N. Prosecutor's View." *The New York Times*, 13 Apr. 2017, https://www.nytimes.com/2017/04/13 /opinion/khmer-rouge-tribunal-a-un-prosecutors-view.html.

THE NEW YORK TIMES. "Persecuted Yazidis Again Caught in Larger Struggle." *The New York Times*, 11 Aug. 2014, https://www.nytimes.com/2014/08/12 /world/middleeast/persecuted-yazidis-again-caught-in-larger-struggle.html.

THE NEW YORK TIMES. "The Persecution of the Rohingya." *The New York Times*, 29 Oct. 2014, https://www.nytimes.com/2014/10/30/opinion/the -persecution-of-the-rohingya.html.

THE NEW YORK TIMES. "The Secret Death Toll of America's Drones." *The New York Times*, 30 Mar. 2019, https://www.nytimes.com/2019/03/30 /opinion/drones-civilian-casulaties-trump-obama.html.

PASCHYN, CHRISTINA M. "Russia Is Trying to Wipe Out Crimea's Tatars." *The New York Times*, 19 May 2016, https://www.nytimes.com/2016/05 /20/opinion/russia-is-trying-to-wipe-out-crimeas-tatars.html.

ROSENBERG, TINA. "For Veterans, a Surge of New Treatments for Trauma." *The New York Times*, 26 Sept. 2012, https://opinionator.blogs.nytimes .com/2012/09/26/for-veterans-a-surge-of-new-treatments-for-trauma/.

RUDD, KEVIN. "Myanmar's Rohingya Crisis Meets Reality." *The New York Times*, 21 Sept. 2017, https://www.nytimes.com/2017/09/21/opinion /myanmar-rohingya-aung-san-suu-kyi.html.

RUDOREN, JODI. "Inside a Jordanian Refugee Camp: Reporter's Notebook." *The New York Times*, 22 Sept. 2015, https://www.nytimes.com/2015/09/22 /insider/inside-a-jordanian-refugee-camp-reporters-notebook.html.

RUDOREN, JODI. "In Torn Gaza, if Roof Stands, It's Now Home." *The New York Times*, 17 Aug. 2014, https://www.nytimes.com/2014/08/18/world /middleeast/gaza-strip-war-leaves-another-crisis-for-displaced-gazans .html.

SCHMITT, ERIC, AND CHARLIE SAVAGE. "Trump Administration Steps Up Air War in Somalia." *The New York Times*, 10 Mar. 2019, https://www.nytimes.com/2019/03/10/us/politics/us-somalia-airstrikes-shabab.html.

SENGUPTA, SOMINI. "Migrant Crisis Raises Issues of Refugees' Rights and Nations' Obligations." *The New York Times*, 23 Sept. 2015, https://www.nytimes.com/2015/09/24/world/europe/migrant-crisis-raises-issues-of-refugees-rights-and-nations-obligations.html.

SHORE, MARCI. "Poland Digs Itself a Memory Hole." *The New York Times*, 4 Feb. 2018, https://www.nytimes.com/2018/02/04/opinion/poland-holocaust-law-justice-government.html.

SPECIA, MEGAN. "How a Nation Reconciles After Genocide Killed Nearly a Million People." *The New York Times*, 25 Apr. 2017, https://www.nytimes.com/2017/04/25/world/africa/rwandans-carry-on-side-by-side-two-decades-after-genocide.html.

SPECIA, MEGAN. "How Syria's Death Toll Is Lost in the Fog of War." *The New York Times*, 13 Apr. 2018, https://www.nytimes.com/2018/04/13/world/middleeast/syria-death-toll.html.

SPECIA, MEGAN. "383,000: Estimated Death Toll in South Sudan's War." *The New York Times*, 26 Sept. 2018, https://www.nytimes.com/2018/09/26/world/africa/south-sudan-civil-war-deaths.html.

THRALL, NATHAN. "The Past 50 Years of Israeli Occupation. And the Next." *The New York Times*, 2 June 2017, https://www.nytimes.com/2017/06/02/opinion/sunday/the-past-50-years-of-israeli-occupation-and-the-next.html.

WALSH, DECLAN. "The Tragedy of Saudi Arabia's War." *The New York Times*, 26 Oct. 2018, https://www.nytimes.com/interactive/2018/10/26/world/middleeast/saudi-arabia-war-yemen.html.

WALSH, DECLAN, AND ERIC SCHMITT. "Arms Sales to Saudis Leave American Footprints on Yemen's Carnage." *The New York Times*, 25 Dec. 2018, https://www.nytimes.com/2018/12/25/world/middleeast/yemen-us-saudi-civilian-war.html.

WOOD, ELISABETH JEAN, AND DARA KAY COHEN. "How to Counter Rape During War." *The New York Times*, 28 Oct. 2015, https://www.nytimes.com/2015/10/29/opinion/how-to-counter-rape-during-war.html.

Index

This book is current up until the time of printing. For the most up-to-date reporting, visit www.nytimes.com.